"Where did you get this horse?" the stranger demanded, striving to choke back his rage.

"L-Let me g-go, y-you uncivil . . . ized . . . b-brute! I m-merely borrowed the horse t-to come on an errand!"

"You lie!" he challenged. "You appropriated it from the Carnleigh stables—"

"H-how dare you accuse me of such a thing!" Diane cried, forgetting for a moment that she was dressed in servants' clothing. And flinging self-control to the winds, she dealt him a resounding smack across his supercilious face with her free hand.

At first she thought he would strike her back, but although he was justifiably enraged, he seemed to be even more astonished, for no common kitchen maid would have dared to do such a thing.

She did not know it then, but this was the beginning of a new life—and a new love.

Subterfuge

———◆◆◆———

A NOVEL BY

Freda Michel

A FAWCETT CREST BOOK • NEW YORK

SUBTERFUGE

THIS BOOK CONTAINS THE COMPLETE TEXT OF
THE ORIGINAL HARDCOVER EDITION.

Published by Fawcett Crest Books, a unit of CBS Publica-
tions, the Consumer Publishing Division of CBS Inc., by
arrangement with Robert Hale Limited

Copyright © 1977 by Freda Michel

ISBN: 0-449-23609-9

Printed in the United States of America

10   9   8   7   6   5   4   3   2   1

One

————— ◆▸ —————

The dainty ormolu clock on the elaborate marble fire-place in the library of Carnleigh Hall, Sussex, chimed eleven, evoking a frown of disapproval from the fifth Earl of Carnleigh who lounged behind a ponderous gold-inlaid mahogany desk, paring with meticulous precision the nails of one elegant beringed hand. A look of concentration marred his arresting, though arrogant, features, while his long dark-brown hair—unpowdered—was curled and styled in a fashionable queue, confined by a huge black bow, and gleamed in the morning sunlight in evidence of regular and fastidious care.

Tossing aside the ivory manicuring implement in growing impatience, he snatched up a legal document currently dated January 1759, scanned the first three lines, then flung it down again to beat a loud rhythmical tattoo upon the desk with his white fingers, his bored gaze travelling round the priceless collection of volumes and paintings which, being the envy of his contemporaries, afforded him a brief satisfaction.

Suddenly the peace was shattered. The mahogany doors burst back on their hinges to admit an anxious footman, clad in the Carnleigh livery, who barely had time to find his voice when he was abruptly silenced by a young gentleman in his wake aged about six and twenty, in a state of half-dress and ferocious temper, who came storming into the room closely followed by another, some two years his junior, draped in an outlandishly embroidered silk dressing-robe.

"All right, Jenkins, we'll announce ourselves!" barked the first, his unprepossessing face flushed in anger as he marched up to the desk with his brother on his heels.

With an obsequious bow the footman retreated swiftly, anticipating another turbulent interview between the Earl and his young headstrong brothers. Neither was he mistaken, for even before the doors had closed on him the two outraged young men had fired the first broadside at their elder brother who, unable to distinguish the gist of their grievance from the cacophony, held up a protesting hand in an attempt to restore order, if not tranquillity. Nevertheless it was quite a minute or two before the angry voices abated and tailed away to heavy indignant breathing.

As they confronted each other difficult would it be indeed to find three brothers at such variance: fair languishing Nicholas whose entire life hung upon the amount of starch in his linen, the position of a patch, or the number of gold buttons adorning his waistcoat; tetchy, stocky-built George whose prime ambition—due to his unimpressive looks—was the abolition of every looking-glass in existence. And finally, the Earl himself, whose placid temperament and air of calm authority quelled many a heated scene in the Shadwick household.

"Confound it, Quentin! Calling us to heel at this infernal hour of the day," expostulated George, unable to keep quiet any longer, "—and in the midst of dressing, what's more!"

"Egad!" put in Nicholas. "What o' the harrowin' indignity I suffered? Dragged bodily from me bed, I was, and for what, prithee?"

With a petulant toss of his long fair curls he struck a dramatic pose, displaying to the utmost advantage his ivory complexion which he boasted was the envy of every female in London, and rivalled only by the delicate porcelain in the family collection.

"Very good, Nicholas. I'm sure you cast Peg Woffington into the shade, but not at present, if you please," requested the Earl with forbearance. "If you will kindly calm yourselves, gentlemen, and be seated,"—he waved them to chairs with a graceful gesture—"I shall endeavour to compensate in some small measure for the untimely disturbance."

"Devil a bit! I still say it can't be that important!" growled George under his breath, striding up and down evidently with no intention of seating himself.

"Y're deuced right, George!" accorded Nicholas, his painstakingly cultivated falsetto raised to its highest pitch. "There was I in the abysmal depths o' despair, sacrificin' me lacerated heart in homage to Petronella Wilchards—"

"If you two will remain silent long enough for me to state my business," cut in the Earl, raising his well modulated voice to be heard, "you may then bandy words from here to Hades with my blessing."

The two reluctantly favoured him with their attention, Nicholas reclining in a brocade upholstered armchair of gilded beechwood and viewing his eldest brother in drowsy contempt, while George ceased his stomping to face the head of the family, looking the epitome of defiance and still very much of the opinion that what brother Quentin had to disclose was nought more vital than the latest addition to his stables.

Well might one wonder where George had been when Mother Nature distributed her endowments to the Shadwick sons. His hair, for example, far from rivalling Nicky's angelic fair, or the Earl's rich brown, came somewhere betwixt the two, a dull mousy shade with an infuriating tendency to curl the wrong way in contradiction of his dictates and curling tongs, for which he was reduced in pocket and pride to wearing the conventional wig. His looks were another thorn of injustice in his side, but nothing compared to the thorn his elder brother constituted, as he not only attracted the females in abundance but had the charm and wit to weaken their resistance, and wealth and position to guarantee an overwhelming conquest. Consequently, the resentment accumulated over the years invariably surged to the fore whenever he was brought face to face with Quentin, he being everything George secretly yearned to be, yet was not.

Slowly, deliberately, Lord Carnleigh sat up to pierce each in turn with his cold grey eyes, generating for the first time a feeling of discomfort in his two problem brothers, who began to harbour suspicions that all was not well. This prompted George to reject the idea of the new thoroughbred, yet was he loth to credit the possibility that Quentin actually intended to resurrect the nauseating topic of his gaming debts again.

"As this is the first time in four months that we have all been established 'neath this roof at one and the same time," the Earl began, nonchalantly brushing a speck from one great silver-laced cuff of sapphire velvet, "I have taken the opportunity to call a family gathering in order to apprise you of certain events about to occur which will affect you directly."

Nicholas gave an inanimate wave, presumably to attract the Earl's attention.

"Well? What is it, Nicholas?" sighed my lord.

"Hem, will ye be long?"

"Yes, dammit!" abetted George. "It's almost noon and I've to be in town by two!"

"I-It's me pea-green satin, d'ye see? Can't shrug m'self into it in ten minutes. Sort o' has t' be negotiated—"

"Ten minutes to don your infernal coat?" expostulated George.

"O' course not, George! Can't be done a minute short o' twenty-three."

"Pardon me for intruding upon such a delicate topic," interposed their brother sardonically. "But I cannot conceive how the mere donning of a coat can be a greater consequence than the question of your future."

"Can't I finish dressing?" persisted George. "Blast it! Fellow could take a chill!"

"Then I suggest you seat yourself nearer the fire, George," advised the Earl, obviously with no intention of allowing his brother out of his sight. "To resume," he went on as George stomped off down the room with a mutinous scowl. "It is my duty to inform you that you are about to experience considerable changes in your position—"

"Yes! Yes! You've said all that, Quen," broke in George impatiently.

"What sort o' changes?" queried Nicholas.

"Changes in fortune," obliged the Earl, evoking gasps of relief from the two though engendered by precisely what, his lordship was temporarily at a loss to know.

"Phew, thank heaven for that!" declared George roundly. "And not before time either, if I may say so, Quentin. Been a sight too tight on the purse-strings! Said it months ago, didn't I, Nicky?"

"Aye, an oath on't, George," drawled Nicholas in languid agreement, showing greater interest in the hang of his dragon-emblazoned robe of Chinese silk. "Recall it quite distinctly. Ye called Quen a stingy, tight-fisted old—"

"Yes, well, we won't go into detail," the other hastily cut in, anxious to preserve cordial relations. "Er—how much do you have in mind, Quentin?" he probed apprehensively. "Hm, let me see . . . two . . . four hundred. . .three thousand and eighty-four . . ." His eyes, of a rare violet shade, transgressed ceilingwards where they remained fixed upon Aphrodite, frolicking with her nymphs, whilst he embarked upon a rapid mental calculation. ". . . something in the region of—hum—nine thousand should set things right,—er—too much to expect, I s'pose?"

"Gadzooks, George! Ye play far too steep!" squawked Nicholas fussing with lace scented handkerchief. "I shall beg a mere five."

"We. . .ll, p'raps I could manage on five at a pinch," grudged George, loth to be too greedy lest he get nothing, and having magnanimously decided that this smaller sum would suffice, sat waiting expectantly for confirmation that he was getting it. But no such confirmation came, goading him to leap afoot and exclaim irritably: "Well, Quentin? Hang me, for a man with something to say you're a devilish time in saying it!"

The Earl repaid him with a look of disdain. "I was not aware that I had yet been granted the opportunity," he remarked dryly.

"Fie on ye, Quentin, for the dull-witted f'low y'are today!" chirruped Nicholas, every whit as anxious as George to know what the round figure was to be. "Poor George! Ye've got him fair sweatin' on number five."

"Then I suggest George sit himself down again for he is about to undergo a considerable shock," responded the Earl, his voice bereft of sympathy.

"Shock!" ejaculated George.

"I knew it! Burn an' blister me, I knew it!" burst out Nicholas. "Plague take ye, Quen! Shouldn't ha' given George a shock like that!"

"He has yet to sustain it," pointed out the Earl significantly. "And I refuse to continue whilst you remain on your feet, George. Should you see fit to turn violent I should be at a decided disadvantage."

"Lud! Don't tell me you're going to cough up nought but a miserly two," groaned George.

"No, George, not two," Lord Carnleigh affirmed benignly. "But you are headed in the right direction."

A gasp erupted from Nicholas. "Y-Ye don't mean we ain't gettin' no increase after all?"

"On the contrary, Nicholas, you an't getting *any* increase," his lordship replied with irony.

"What! No increase?"

"No, George. And what is more—"

"Th-There's worse?" stammered Nicholas, weakly.

"Impossible!" snapped George. "What could be worse than getting no increase?"

The Earl lounged back in his capacious winged

chair, a half-smile playing round the solitary patch adorning the corner of his mouth.

"I should say, my dear George, having to suffer a substantial *decrease*."

"D-Decrease!" screeched Nicholas.

"'S death! If 'tis not another of his infernal ruses!" rasped George, upon regaining his speech. "Never could fathom your blighted sense of humour, Quen."

"Ecod, ye can't, Quentin!" remonstrated Nicholas, realising his eldest brother might be issuing no empty threat, if the peculiar sensation in his stomach was to be relied upon. "Ye can't treat us in such shabby fashion, damme!"

"Can't I, Nicky? I assure you, I have not the slightest intention of settling your exorbitant debts out of my personal fortune any longer."

"Oh, good gad, not that again!" lamented George.

"Your pecuniary position is grave, extremely so." The warning in the Earl's voice suddenly belied his nonchalant manner.

"Fustian! You're exaggerating, Quen," exclaimed George with a nervous laugh. "It can't be that bad—c-can it?"

The Earl's eyes narrowed. "You do not regard a bundle of promissory notes totalling some twelve thousand guineas anything to be unduly concerned about?"

The hang-dog George shrugged non-committally, wondering how his brother had come by the information, while Nicholas huddled for refuge in his chair, his innocent blue eyes swivelling from one brother to the other.

"Blast it, Quen! Even if I have ploughed through the fifty thousand father left me, I still have mother's allowance, not to mention Uncle Dryden's twenty thousand," vituperated George, rankled at being made to feel a midget just because he happened to have been born four years later than the head of the house.

The Earl heaved a sign of resignation. "It distresses me to tell you, George, but they expired, all three, over two years agone."

"I don't believe it! Tar and feather me, if I do!"

"Two years and five months, to be exact. And Nicky's,"—here a disarming smile at the gawping Nicholas, "last April."

"I protest! 'Tis all a confounded hoax!" cried Nicholas, much affronted.

"Call it divination if you will," the Earl went on, trying to make himself heard once again. "However, anticipating some dissension, I had the foresight to have accounts drawn up." He paused to extract two lengthy documents from the drawer on his right, which he then proffered to his sceptical brothers. "One for you, George, listing your drinking and gaming debts to date. And one for you, Nicholas, to your wine, women and tailor."

The documents were pounced upon and scrutinised in awesome silence whilst Lord Carnleigh casually availed himself of a generous pinch of snuff from an intricately carved ivory snuff-box picked out in gold.

" 'S blood!" George was first to expostulate. "I can't have exploded a hundred and twenty thousand in— how many years? Six?"

"Five," amended the Earl, consulting his impressive array of calculations. "And the precise figure is—as you will see if you cast your eyes a trifle farther down—one hundred and fifty-seven thousand, three hundred and forty-eight pounds, fourteen shillings and two pence."

"Eh? Thirty-seven thousand I owe you? Added to the twelve I owe the duns—view-halloo!"

"Correction. Forty-nine thousand you owe me," the Earl enlightened him, pocketing his snuff-box. "Do close your mouth, George. The view from my position is aught but inspiring."

"Y-You a-actually settled my debts, Quen?" he managed to stammer, stunned. "A-All twelve thousand g-guineas?"

Lord Carnleigh inclined his dark immaculate head with marked condescension.

George did not quite know what to say as he gaped thunderstruck at the Earl, frantically debating how he ought to express his overwhelming gratitude.

"Ex-Extremely good of you, Quentin, by gad it is!" he gasped anon. "Don't know what to say . . . b-but you'll get it all back—every penny of it, even if it takes a lifetime!"

The Earl was not impressed. "Unfortunately I am not prepared to wait that long, George," he drawled disinterestedly. "You have a period of six months."

The silence was almost deafening, before George exploded into guffaws of laughter—to Nicky's bewildered concern, who at once suspected that the calamitous news was having an adverse effect upon his brain.

"Thunder and turf, what a jester!" he eventually panted between guffaws. "Always did have a nimble wit, eh, Nicky?"

"A period of six months, for both of you," emphasized the Earl.

"M-Me?" wailed Nicholas.

"Yes, Nicholas," affirmed the Earl, referring once again to his accounts. A round sum of thirty-four thousand, nine hundred and fifty-two pounds, to be paid by July, twenty-first."

The humour suddenly vanished from George's face.

"Stop gullin us, Quen! The jesting's over!"

Lord Carnleigh leaned forward, a glint of menace in his steady gaze.

"Your debts are no jesting matter," he flung back with blistering sarcasm. "Neither is my ultimatum. I repeat, you have six months in which to pay every outstanding penny, or you pack up your effects and go."

"Go?" echoed Nicholas, bobbing up with a start.

"Rot me, you know as well as I that we could never repay those sums in a lifetime," snapped George, harshly.

"Not in your present circumstances, mayhap. However, if I might venture a suggestion which could resolve—"

"Yes! Yes! Anything!" burst out Nicholas.

"And what might that be?" prompted George, devoured with suspicion.

The Earl paused to consult his silver ruby-set pocket watch with infuriating deliberation, comparing the hour with the clock upon the mantelshelf before returning the watch to his pocket and responding laconically:

"Marriage."

"M-Marriage?" spluttered George.

"Devil take ye, Quen! Ye really ought t' guard y'r tongue," protested Nicholas. "Just look at poor George. Gone as white as a baker's apron."

Sympathetic would be the last word to describe the Earl's expression as he resumed.

"As I myself am obliged to marry I fail to see why—"

"You? Y-You are about to get wed? Well!"

breathed George much easier, wiping an arm across his fevered brow. "That's wonderful news, Quen! Isn't it, Nicky?"

"Zounds! Wonderful!" supported Nicholas, leaping afoot to join brother George in felicitating the Earl who was not a little taken aback by the force of their enthusiasm.

"Heartiest congratulations, Quen!" gushed George, pumping the Earl's arm up and down. "Who's the lucky female? Who's to be future Countess of Carnleigh, eh? Felicity Frogmorton, p'raps? No?—er—Selina Stiggins, then?"

"Or Teresa Wimpole?" volunteered Nicholas.

The Earl returned a dumbfounded stare. "You appreciate that you will both be obliged to find alternative abodes?"

"Yes, we understand all right, don't we, Nicky?"

"O' course, George! Not lunatics, Quen. Perfectly lucid. Y're gettin' wed. Wife moves in, we move out."

"If I may make so bold," observed the Earl, eyeing them with grave scepticism. "You are both taking it extremely flippant."

"Why not?" parried George.

"Aye," abetted Nicholas. "Not the end o' the world, m' dear f'low, just because ye decide t' don the shackles."

"May I ask where you intend to go?" queried their brother, curiously.

"Hm, early days yet," replied George, pensively stroking his unshaven chin. "Probably Croxton, or Wynlands. They're both within travelling distance of the Capital."

"Ah! I see you plan the Grand Tour of my estates. Loth as I am to disappoint you—"

"Aw, Quen, don't be so selfish," complained Nicholas. "Ye can't live in all the deuced houses at once."

"You shall have a modest allowance until the end of the season by which time you must have found yourselves heiresses—"

"You're intoxicated!"

"Y're jokin'!"

"As you very well know, George, I am never intoxicated. And marriage, Nicky, is nothing to joke about."

George rapped out an oath. "You won't get me to the altar! Not if all the duns in hell were on my heels! I'll be damned if I'm chaining myself to some rich priggish brat with a face enough to curdle the morning milk!"

"Whom you wed, of course, is entirely your own affair," observed the Earl, blandly. "But you either chain yourself to a female of fortune, or a dark dank prison cell. The choice is yours."

"Ecod, Quentin! Ye can't do it, ye can't!" cried Nicholas, his pallor turning two shades lighter. "Not t' y'r own flesh an' blood! Damme, 'tis pos'tively uncivilised!"

The Earl slammed his desk and rose to his feet. "You think I should stand by and let you continue unchecked in your reckless conduct? Squandering my fortune and inheritance until my entire estate is forfeit and I end up alongside you?" he thundered angrily.

As Lord Carnleigh's anger waxed, George's waned. He had never before seen his elder brother so passionately roused. He and Nicky had run up debts, yes, there had always been debts, but Quentin had always stumped up without much ado after the usual scolding and dissertation on the folly of their ways. Evidently this time was going to be rather different, but no doubt

he would come about in the end, if he and Ricky
played their cards with discretion.

In preparation to plead his cause, George rose
gingerly, squared his broad shoulders, cleared his
throat and gave a nervous tug at his crumpled linen,
while the craven Nicholas crouched silent in his chair,
nurturing a forlorn hope that his presence would be
overlooked as he peered cautiously through his long
hair at the Earl's stern countenance.

"Er—Quentin," wheedled George, striving to humble
himself. "Please would you p'raps give us another
chance? I-It will never happen again, I promise on
oath."

"No!" came the inexorable reply. "I have rescued
the pair of you from Debtors' Alley for the last time.
The warning is final! It is high time you took yourselves hence in search of wives wealthy enough to indulge your extravagant tastes. I need not remind you
that I am under the greatest obligation of all to suffer
wedlock. However, I adamantly refuse to suffer it
whilst I yet have your greedy grasping fingers clawing
into mine inheritance! I leave tomorrow for Italy. In
six months I shall return—with my future bride!"

With that he made to leave but Nicholas detained
him, somehow unable to reconcile himself to his
brother's intended nuptials.

"Y're goin' through with it, Quen? Y're truly gettin'
wed?"

The Earl returned a raised eyebrow. "You appear to
hold the holy estate in some aversion, Nicholas, like
consuming a dose of physic."

"N-No, no. 'Tis just that it's—er—a trifle unexpected."

"The responsibility of wedlock stables a man, ma-

tures him, gives him something—or rather someone—
to live for other than himself. It enables him to get life
in its true perspective, and appreciate that it is not all
gaming, drinking and wenching."

"Huh! No point in getting wed if you feel like that
about it," muttered George, sourly.

Two pairs of resentful eyes followed the Earl's tall
graceful figure to the doors where he paused, turning
his mocking gaze upon them.

"Should I return to find you both in the same impecunious state and without a well-endowed petticoat
in the wind, then I am loth to say, gentlemen, that
you will find yourselves within the hour, revelling in
the delightful hospitality of the Fleet."

And with a travesty of a bow he retired, leaving his
brothers to ponder his grim prognostication.

Two

As predicted, Lord Carnleigh departed betimes the following morning with his large retinue. Thus George and Nicholas were left to their own devices, and whereas the latter advocated losing not a moment in obeying Quentin's explicit commands, George laughed his elder brother's threats aside, assuring the dubious Nicky that the nuptial noose was *not* the only way out of their financial straits and that it was certainly not encompassing his neck if there were any help for it. All it required was a little mental application and he, if not Nicholas, would concoct a brilliant scheme before long.

Nicholas, however, was not wholly averse to the noose encompassing his neck as long as it were to be placed there by his adored Petronella. But soon he was basking in the rays of George's optimism so effectively that ere he realised it two clear months had lapsed.

Howbeit, as spring returned so did Nicky's apprehension which he at once communicated to George, who grudgingly confessed that he had not yet thought of anything and needed still more time. Another conference was called to consider every avenue of escape, including pledging the family heirlooms, squeezing further loans from creditors and, in desperation, some kind of employment, but each avenue terminated with a major hindrance.

No, according to George's inveterate gaming instinct, only one agreeable course remained open to them and that was to take what money they had up to London, and in the ebullient heat of the season hazard their luck at the gaming tables. But long ere George had finished making the proposal Nicholas was shrieking his objection to it, pronouncing George the worst gamester in Christendom. In this stalemate situation, all George had to do was point out that there was more than a remote possibility of Nicholas spying his fair Petronella.

As far as Nicholas was concerned no more needed to be said. And so, all trinkets, rings, fobs, patch and snuff-boxes were gathered together, large in number though modest in value, tempting the brothers to include one or two expendable items belonging to the Earl. The sum total these were expected to realise was somewhere in the region of six thousand pounds— ample for their purpose.

Without more ado, bags were packed and a messenger dispatched to the City to alert the servants at the Earl's town house in Hanover Square of their impending arrival. Nicholas was heard to cavil at staying at Quentin's house bethinking he might return unexpectedly and catch them unawares, but as they could not possibly afford to rent rooms elsewhere—even should they be available—found himself obliged to concur.

Late that evening saw the two established in London partaking of supper whilst planning the expenditure of their modest wealth. Every penny was to be speculated at the tables with the exception of a mere ten pounds or so needed for incidental expenses, decided George, who lost no time in arranging their first venture abroad for that very night. Nicholas was in full agreement until the moment came to depart when he suddenly cried off, declaring he did not feel quite up to it and was about to be seized by the vapours at the mere thought of his very life and cherished hopes of marrying Petronella draining away over the green baize, for George was destined to lose, and nothing king nor devil could say would convince him otherwise.

Hot on the heels of this upset came a bitter dispute about the precise amount to be gamed in this initial experiment. Understandably George, having more faith in his gaming prowess than his brother, was firmly in favour of staking all in one fell swoop, but Nicholas was equally adamant in wanting to limit the sum of two hundred pounds lest they lose all. And as neither would relent the first venture ended up with George rampaging off to drink himself to death at the nearest alehouse, whilst Nicholas gave licence to his vapours in Hanover Square.

Thus, their first week in London was expended in an atmosphere of strained silence with neither prepared to give ground, while George's resentment waxed with each passing day, aware that time was running out, apart from which if he imbibed much more liquor his brain should be too pickled to concentrate on anything. Consequently, though it pained him sorely, he acceded to Nicky's whim and consented to uphold any stipulations he cared to make concerning the distribution of their meagre funds, more meagre than anticipated due to their collection of trinkets not having realised anything resembling six thousand pounds, but instead, a niggardly three thousand six hundred and eighty.

Therefore, the following evening George swallowed his chagrin and accepted the two hundred pounds from

Nicholas with civility, if not gratitude, and bore himself swiftly off to his haunt in St. James's Street, clutching the money avidly to his wine-spattered waistcoat. Once again, Nicholas elected to languish at home rather than be party to the dire fate in store, and retired to bed to bury his head in his goose-feather pillow, his state of penury preventing him venturing forth to solicit the company of his beloved Petronella, who was accustomed to having her expensive tastes indulged to the full. He tossed and turned in his bed, listening with half an ear to the external hubbub of the great city as the underworld came to life, and the hourly cry of the watch who trudged by with flickering flambeau and grating rattle calling—eleven . . . twelve . . . one . . .

Nicholas heard no more as he fell asleep, to be rudely awakened at four in the morning by George who showered something very akin to golden guineas upon his bed and which sleepy-eyed Nicholas dismissed as the most realistic dream he had ever experienced. But come the morning, when one was sufficiently sober and the other sufficiently alert, the guineas were counted and the total of one thousand, seven hundred and fifty-two arrived at.

It is perhaps, small wonder that his beginner's luck flew to George's head like a flagon of heady cider, urging him to be off again the next night anticipating even bigger gains with the princely sum of five hundred guineas which he had extracted with minimal difficulty from Nicholas.

So elated was Nicholas by this unexpected improvement in his fortune that he decided to act upon it, though somewhat prematurely, and venture forth to declare himself to the object of his heart, and convey to her the wonderful news.

Having arrived at this momentous decision he then expended three hours closeted with his man, preparing himself with more than his customary niceness for the occasion and, anon, emerged duly powdered, painted and patched, his slender boyish frame clothed in a floral silk waistcoat 'neath a full skirted coat of sky blue brocade, with snowy lace frothing at chin and wrists and clocks adorning his white silk stockings. His toilet was completed with a liberal sprinkling of flower water following which he donned a purple cloak lined with shagreen silk, perched his Nivernois hat at a jaunty angle upon his powdered curls, and sallied forth to call upon his lady with a four-foot beribboned cane in one hand and a pomander in the other.

With the high red heels of his paste buckled shoes tapping confidently upon the stone steps he descended to the cobbled street where he hailed a chair and commanded the chairmen to bear him swiftly to Mount Street. Upon arrival at number six Nicholas requested to be set down, paid his reckoning, and approached the imposing door of his amour with all the grace and dignity he could summon, aware that she might well be observing from a window. Neither, apparently, was he mistaken, for as he was about to tap upon the door with his cane a sudden movement of the curtain upstairs caught his eye, and ere his cane made contact the door was wrenched open and a neat mob-capped maid was curtsying him over the threshold, urging him, in respectful undertones and with an anxious glance up and down the street, to make great haste lest he was spied.

Nicholas's heartbeat quickened considerably at such an eager reception though he found it somewhat deflating to his ego that his Petronella should be loth to have his presence known. However, he was to be given excellent reason for this ere long, and without more ado he was guided up two flights of stairs and into an elegant boudoir hung with pink and white damask, the whole atmosphere redolent with the intoxicating scent of his adored one which immediately flew to his head.

But most intoxicating of all was Petronella herself who at this moment appeared in the doorway from her dresssing-closet where she remained awhile, poised like a dainty butterfly, a vision in misty white gauze with her long auburn hair flowing about her young shoulders, a vision which spellbound Nicholas to such a degree that he was at once oblivious to all else—to the maid relieving him of cloak, hat and cane and retiring to an ante-room, leaving the two discreetly alone.

"N-Nicky?" breathed Petronella, as if seeking to reassure herself that it was really he.

"Pet. . .ron. . .ella," gasped Nicholas, taking two steps forward, which seemed to be all he could manage at this present time.

"Every single night I have waited, hoped, longed, ever since last we met. A-And if one hopes long enough, hard enough . . . I am told it . . . it . . ." On impulse she ran across the room as if about to throw herself bodily into his arms, sending Nicky's brain reeling madly as he half extended his arms to receive her—when she pulled up short two feet away, her sense of decorum suddenly excelling her heart as she self-consciously averted her face, a face of classic beauty, well-defined, with a flawless complexion, and set with eyes of a profound blue which played havoc with Nicky's self-control. Instead, she rested a delicate pink hand, childlike, upon his brocade sleeve and guided him over to a high-backed settee by the fire-place where, before she could remove her hand Nicholas seized it and pressed it fervently to his lips, determined to kiss some part of her lest he fall prostrate at her feet with unquenched desire.

"M-My dearest P-Petron. . .ella," stammered Nicholas, drugged by her beauty and close proximity. "I-I could not bring m'self to call until m' circumstances allowed. Faith, how could I stay away from such overwhelmin' beauty as thine? 'Pon my life, I've thought and dreamt o' nought else these weeks past! Ecod! M' soul's no longer me own. Y're an enchantress, a sorceress, to bedevil me so!"

She blushed attractively, lowering her eyes as if unaccustomed to receiving such compliments, which Nicholas refused to credit.

"I hear tell, you have earned a considerable reputation with the ladies, Nicholas. . .very many. . .ladies . . . Nicholas?"

As it was more a question than a statement Nicholas felt obliged to volunteer an answer.

"Hem, well, mayhap one or two. But heed not all ye hear, m' love. Scandal is wont to exaggerate other people's foibles."

"Ladies like myself?"

"Nay, never! Forsooth, none like you, Petronella!"

"Y-You. . .l-love me, Nicholas?" she murmured coyly.

"Love ye! Gad! More than words can say. Put me t' the test! Anythin'! I'll fling m'self into the deepest ocean! Leap from the Bloody Tower—er—if ye'll pardon me—"

"You would do all that, for m-me?"

"Zounds, Petronella! I'd give me very life for ye."

She seemed to be content with this and returned an

ardent smile, until she suddenly recalled something and looked downcast.

"Our meeting must be kept a closely guarded secret, Nicky. M-My father has f-forbidden me to resume our ac-acquain. . .tance." Her voice broke on a tremulous note.

"Fie on't. I beg ye not t' languish so, m' sweet love," besought Nicholas, distraught by her anguish. "For what reason does he object?" he questioned superfluously, for he himself was able to think of several without undue strain upon his ingenuity.

"I-I cannot say," she turned away to conceal her discomposure, but not far that Nicholas could not still cling to her hand. "I-It would cause you p-pain . . ."

Nicholas shot up erect. "Gad! Whate'er it be, dear one, it must be said m' family ranks wi' the highest in the land."

She sat with golden head lowered, twisting the loveknots adorning her gown into tiny balls, and at length capitulated with a sigh.

"My f-father, Sir Jason, claims you to be lacking in substance, without prospect of title and estate. But it matters not at all to me, Nicholas!" she burst out, fervently. "You must believe that, truly."

She raised her troubled eyes to his, her fingers returning the warmth of his grasp, all of which served to convince him better than all the words in the King's English of her sincerity of heart.

Though he tried to conceal it, Nicky's spirits sank to the toes of his buckled shoes. He could scarcely own Sir Jason's objection unjust. After all, but for George's exceptional luck at the tables the night before, Quentin's grim threat might well have come to pass and he found himself languishing in Fleet Prison before the hunting season. Indeed, what Sir Jason's opinion of him as a prospective son-in-law should then have been something Nicholas did not particularly care to reflect upon.

" 'S life," repined he, shoulders adroop despite his efforts to rally himself. "A title's out o' the question, I'm afraid. But I am an Honourable, Petronella," he perked up hopefully. "Wouldn't that do?"

She shook her head forlornly.

"Curse it! 'Tis an unjust world, an' no mistake," he lamented. "There's m' brother Quentin not only an Earl and Right Honourable, but with a string o' titles in reserve which he'll never get round t' usin' and flourishin' estates t' go with 'em, and all the family wealth, t'boot! Humph," he sighed. "S'pose he could meet an untimely fate in a Venetian canal, but damme, there's George! Could scarce count on two—"

"Nicholas, stop!" cried his lady in alarm, for this was quite alien to his generous nature. "You must not talk so, it's wicked! I forbid you to think such dreadful things, and about your own dear brother, too."

"Forgive me, dear heart! I crave y'r forgiveness, that I, the lowliest creature on God's earth, should cause ye one moment's pain," he supplicated at her beslippered feet. "Oh, Petronella! Why couldn't I ha' met ye when I was a gentleman o' means? Ye gods! O'er an hundred thousand squandered in reckless abandon, and for what, prithee?"

"Don't feel discouraged, Nicholas," she urged him, trying to meet his anguished eyes. "If my father should prevail upon me to wed Lord Pottle, even beat me, I should—"

"Lord *who?*"

"Pottle, Peregrine Pottle—"

" 'Odsbobs, ye can't wed that Jack-puddin'!"

"My father says I must because he is a Viscount, Nicholas, but I shan't! Never! No matter if he were to be made King Pottle!"

"W-Would ye wed m-me, Petronella?" breathed Nicholas, stricken with ardour, unconsciously manoeuvring himself closer.

"Oh yes, Nicky! Yes! This very moment if it were possible!" she blurted out impulsively, turning to him as if offering herself but as Nicholas made to passionately avail himself of the gesture she suffered a pang of conscience as before, and shrank away again, reddening profusely.

Nicholas passed a shaking hand across his moist forehead, wondering how much more of this emotional see-saw he could endure, and if he ought not to take his leave lest his passion run rampant and he did something to warrant her disapproval.

Suddenly he thought of George, though why his irascible brother should pervade his thoughts at this tender moment would be difficult to estimate. Was he winning? Losing? Would he himself be in sufficient funds by the end of the week, month, to be able to return to his beautiful sweet Petronella and beg her hand honourably of her father? Nicholas cursed inwardly to think that his entire future happiness rested solely upon the turn of a mere playing card.

He turned back to his inamorata, though equally unable to meet her eye as she was to meet his.

"Petronella," he began, hoarsely. "Circumstances prevent me declarin' m'self formally at this time. Hows'mever, I anticipate a decided improvement very soon—"

"Oh, Nicky! How wonderful! Simply wonderful!" cried she, clapping her hands in delight.

"Er—ye think if this were to come about y'r father might feel disposed t' regard m' suit in more favourable vein?"

"Yes! Yes! I'm sure it would make all the difference in the world, Nicky! Y-You have good prospects?"

"One might say that, though 'tis not absolutely certain. A possibility, perchance, in a month or so . . ."

Nicholas did not choose to enlarge upon this by venturing into the precarious details of how, where and precisely when he was to come by his fortune lest he blight his loved one's hopes, and her touching faith in him.

"But it will come true, Nicky, I just know it will!" she thrilled, bouncing up and down with glee. "I shall break the news to my father this very night upon his return."

"D'ye think it circumspect, m' love?" demurred Nicholas, loth to be a kill-joy yet anxious to prevent her ruining all. "I mean, I mayn't succeed."

"Oh, you will, Nicky! You will! *Please* say you will? I could never love anyone else, never! An-And if y-you don't m-marry m-me, my N-Nicky," she went on, tearfully, searching frantically for her handkerchief, "I shall be f-forced to m-marry Lord P-Pottle, and y-you wouldn't wish . . . m-me to be . . . burdened with a . . . name like that f-for . . . the rest of . . . m-my life, w-would you? Petronella Pottle," she wailed, "it's even w-worse than . . . W-Wilchards." And to Nicky's disconcertment she burst into floods of tears.

What could a gentleman do but his best to comfort his lady in such dire distress?—which Nicholas did not hesitate to do, to find, ere he had time to blink, Petron-

ella's warm pulsating shapeliness enveloped in his
arms, though he knew not how, with her radiantly
beautiful face submerged in his shoulder, and strands
of her silken hair caressing his shaven cheek. His heart
reeled madly, for never before this night had he made
physical contact with this goddess of his heart, and to
have her there, in his arms, clinging to him as if she
would never let him go, excelled his wildest dreams,
being infinitely more than he had dared hope for upon
this their very first time alone. Indeed, he estimated if
he were to be hanged for it on the morrow it should
have been well worth the sacrifice. George simply *had*
to win!

Deeming himself a Prince among Men for having
achieved so much in but a single hour made Nicholas
firm in his intent not to venture a step further, yet,
found his lips lightly brushing her hair . . . her delicate
ear . . . her wet cheek, and upon raising her tear-
stained face from his shoulder—her exceedingly willing
lips. Willing, eager, then passionate. Nicholas marvelling to find the heat of her ardour just as intense as
his own although he reasoned it must have been her
first profound emotional experience, for alternating
with the bursts of eagerness to volunteer herself were
moments of acute shyness engendered by a genuine
fear for her chastity, and at times she was so childlike
in her innocence and trust that the instincts of a gentleman—which had never troubled him hitherto—forbad
him taking advantage, yet he was quite well aware that
with minimal persuasion she would yield to the ultimate sacrifice and crumble to his will.

How he managed to restrain his raging desire was
something Nicholas would never know, when every instinct was inciting him to do otherwise and gainsay his

remnants of conscience, most of all the huge four-poster bed behind which continually beckoned them into its comforting embrace to partake of the pleasures it had to offer. Indeed, even the Earl himself, that paragon of self-control, would have highly commended his young brother upon his stringent efforts.

Petronella trembled in his arms. Nicholas trembled too, yet at a loss to know why when he must surely have kissed more women in his life than he had inhaled grains of snuff, but never, never like . . . this . . .

"Oh, Pet. . .ron. . .ella," he groaned, delirious with her nearness and the fact that she was clad in little else but her flimsy gauze and lace, free of whale-boned stays and hoops. "Ecod! How ye torture me."

"Y-You love me, Nicky. . .v-very much?" she probed again, her eyes shining with adoration.

"More than me very soul! More than anythin', t' the point o' madness!"

"And you will come again, soon?"

"At dawn tomorrow," he breathed, striving to regain his senses, as she wriggled out of his hold with a giggle.

"Tomorrow evening at eight will be more convenient, and safe. Come, Nicky," she urged him in earnest, summoning her maid with a tinkling silver bell. "It is almost ten o'clock. My father may return at any moment. You must agree that it would not do at all for him to find you here in such a compromising situation?"

Nicholas took his leave, promising on pain of death to be with her on the morrow at prompt eight. He could scarcely recall his return to Hanover Square, so buoyant were his spirits after witnessing the most incredible miracle of his life. Petronella's love maturing before his eyes. Nothing was permitted to alloy this

Elysian dream, no, not even the possibility that George might well have failed upon his second attempt to procure sufficient riches to ransom them from the jaws of disaster.

But George had not failed. On the contrary, he had proved even more successful than the previous night and once again intruded upon his brother's slumbers during the early hours to acquaint him with the fact by showering more guineas upon his bed than Nicholas had ever seen, and which the two rejoiced over till long after dawn.

So delighted was Nicholas at this outcome that the following evening George was granted the unprecedented sum of three thousand guineas to hazard at the table, whilst Nicholas again prinked and preened himself, but this time to solicit the hand of his future wife. For the momentous occasion he selected his best suit of amber satin edged with gold lace, and a black camlet cloak with silver frogs, lined with amber shalloon; the customary white ruffles flounced at chin and wrists, and though he retained the pomander the malacca cane was relinquished in favour of a silver-hilted dress sword.

With his heart thumping like the martial drum-beat of an army marching into battle Nicholas arrived at number six Mount Street as the parish clock chimed eight, and was somewhat dismayed to find all in darkness with not a solitary light at the windows nor even the necessary flambeau in its sconce upon the wall. Consequently, long before he rapped upon the door misgivings were gnawing at his inside and, sure enough, found them justified when there came no response.

Gone! She was gone! The light of his life was extinguished like the flambeau and now he not only bodily but spiritually floundered in darkness, a darkness of excruciating despair. Suddenly he was seized by a towering rage and hammered upon the offending door with every means at his disposal thus seeking to relieve, in some small measure, his agony of soul.

However, although the street boasted not a single passerby, this display of temperament did not fail to attract some attention, and he felt an unexpected tug at his cloak.

Nicholas leapt back with a start to view the intruder who presumed to lay hands upon him, his sword glinting in the moonlight, drawn, ready to strike, but at sight of the tattered object by his side he sheathed the weapon again.

"Fie! Be off with ye, grubby urchin!" admonished Nicholas with a rebuking gesture. "Away 'fore I call the constable, damme!"

"Be ye the 'igh-flyin' cove, sir?" queried the boy, undaunted by Nicky's hostile display.

"Be I?" parried Nicholas, viewing the other askance.

" 'Ave a messidge fer yer honour"—sniff—"from a foine leddy what lives 'ere, if yer honour 'appens to be"—sniff—"the 'on . . . olbable Nich . . . erlas . . ."

"Yes! Yes! I be—er—am he," acknowledged Nicholas, waxing impatient. "What is't? Come along, wretch, state y'r business and ha' done wi' the games! And keep y'r confounded distance," he added, administering pomander to his nose as he took a hasty step in retreat. "I am plagued wi' squeamish nostrils and y'r distinctive odour offends 'em."

"The leddy axed me t' give this 'ere note"—sniff—"to the—the—On . . . ourl . . . bable—"

"Yes. I've heard all that! Just give me the note and be off with ye!" snapped Nicholas peevishly, making to

seize the note to find it swiftly substituted by an extended grimy palm.

"It be a mortal cold night, yer honour, sir," hastened
to point out the child, keeping a tactful distance.

Despite the time of year Nicholas had to agree that
the air had developed a chill, or was it on account of
his sad loss?

"Very well," capitulated he, dropping a shilling into
the little cold hand. "But hail me a chair 'fore ye go.
I've little wish t' run foul o' the Mohocks!"

The chair was hailed forthwith and the boy vanished.

Here, Nicholas found to his further disconcertment
that, due to the deficiency of light and his lady's flam-
boyant hand, he was unable to absorb the contents of
the note until he arrived in Hanover Square, when he
fled to the sanctity of his rooms and anxiously unfolded
the scented vellum to read written thereon, rather tremulously:

Dearest Love,
    Alas! I fear we are quite undone! Last Evening I
revealed our Cherished Hopes to my dear papa who
took it all extremely Ill, despite your expected improvement in Fortune which I did convey to him in
the Pleasantest Terms, yet which he did choose to
Disbelieve. He seeks to part us for ever, Beloved One,
and has Banished me to my Aunt Emiline in Biggleswade who is the worst Creature imaginable and will
keep me to my Room upon Watery Gruel until I
renounce my Love for you. This I will never do. I
shall Love you always, my Nicky,
                              Yr own adoring
                              Petronella.

Nicholas pressed the vellum feverishly to his lips

then read it through again, refolded it, and pocketed it over his heart before prostrating himself upon a daybed to grieve over his lady's absence and ruminate the problem of how to realise his burning ambition under threat of this catastrophic development. Obviously, his immediate reaction was to leap to horse and gallop non-stop all the way to Biggleswade to rescue his damsel, but what should he do with her after that? He could scarcely take her to Carnleigh Hall. Furthermore, it would be courting downright disaster to leave George to his own reckless devices in London. No, Nicholas decided to postpone his lady's rescue a week or two. After all, she was in safe keeping with her aunt and out of reach of this Peregrine Pottle, therefore, the situation did not warrant drastic action, as yet. Besides, his fortune was waxing stronger day by day and very soon he would be a gentleman of considerable consequence, someone to be reckoned with—even by Sir Jason Wilchards.

To Nicky's continued delight George's luck held, and whereas the handsome profits of the first two ventures were never surpassed, nor even equalled, it was found nevertheless, at the end of two weeks that their mutual assets amounted to almost thirty thousand pounds! But suddenly their fortune ceased to wax. Granted, neither did it wane, not at once. It was a few days later following a period of stagnation that the erosion began, a small loss at first yet it filled George with dismay.

Had he managed to retain his composure and confide the misfortune to Nicholas instead of trying to conceal it by sacrificing good guineas to recoup bad, all might have been well. But, alas, this loss was followed by others, gathering momentum and size until Nicholas, whose amorous intrigue had consumed his mind to the exclusion of all else including the prize money, discovered to his abject horror that he and George were worth the outstanding sum of one hundred and twenty-nine pounds, five shillings and threepence-farthing.

It was hardly surprising that Nicholas forbad George another groat, and ranted and raved at him that he had done nought but confirm his own original opinion of him as a gamester, bemoaning the fact that Petronella was now lost to him for ever. And although George persisted in the dogma that he still had time and wherewithal to recoup his losses and acquire the sum needed to pay Quentin, Nicholas remained adamant, now intending to invest the meagre amount left in some mercantile venture, and meanwhile, crave Quentin's clemency a little longer.

George capitulated to Nicholas with an actual apology, or so it appeared, and suggested they pack up and leave London on the morrow, there now being no reason to stay even if they could afford to. But nothing was further from George's mind which Nicholas discovered to his cost upon waking soon after four in the morning, aghast to find the entire sum of money gone from his trinket box and George's bed deserted and undisturbed.

Never had George's return been awaited with such fervour as it was by Nicholas that morn. And when the black sheep finally did appear, with the sun well positioned in the sky and the deflating news that he had lost everything they possessed, Nicholas flew at him in hysteria. Both kept to their rooms throughout the following day and rose in time for supper that evening, during which George made several attempts to exonerate himself but, each time, he met with a curt rebuff from Nicholas. Indeed, why Nicky troubled to quit his bed at all was something George failed to comprehend for he was back in it again upon abandoning the table, after devouring not a solitary morsel.

Thus, with purse drained and rejected by his brother, George whiled away the night before the cold empty grate, seeking consolation in bottle after bottle of the Earl's best burgundy. He did not reproach Nicholas for feeling the way he did. He readily agreed that there was no one to blame but himself for frittering away their last hope of salvation, which knowledge served only to aggravate his ill-humour the more. It seemed incredible that he had actually held thirty thousand pounds in his own hands but a short while ago, and that it now no longer existed.

George gaped like an imbecile down at his offending hands as if half expecting the money to miraculously reappear and save him from his fate, fettered to a wife—or Fleet Prison!

Three

By mid-afternoon the following day George was as sober as he ever would be, therefore, it was mutually decided betwixt the two brothers that they depart for their Sussex home.

The journey, a mere three hours at a good spanking pace, took six due to Nicky's delicate state of health, for he had not obtained a wink of sleep and averred that his entire body would crumble to pieces if the cattle proceeded at more than a fast walk. The invalid lay prone upon the purple plush seat with his fair head supported by a lavender cushion, alternating laced handkerchief with aromatic bottle to his sensitive nostrils, while George rode up on the box alongside the coachman, partly to escape Nicholas, and partly in the hope that the fresh April breeze would clear his befuddled brain.

Upon arrival at Carnleigh Hall, at ten o'clock, the martyred Nicholas rallied himself sufficiently to proceed indoors on his own two legs, and up to his chambers upon the second floor. Here, he remained cloistered for the subsequent five days, unable to establish if he were more desolate at the loss of his adorable Petronella, or the damning prospect of the debtors' cell which now loomed on his horizon as invitable as the Day of Judgment. Recrimination, in goodly measure, was heaped upon the head of George whom Nicholas deemed the worst brother anyone could have, which generated the thought that such an one might sink to the unscrupulous depths of snatching his beloved Petronella from under his nose if he was not careful and kept a vigilant eye on him.

It was precisely this which finally persuaded Nicholas to vacate his bed with some alacrity, for he could hardly keep a vigilant eye upon his brother whilst languishing in his bed in the farthermost wing of the house. Indeed, such haste did he make in completing his toilet that he was descending the stairs within half an hour, quite surprising himself, and utterly dumfounding his valet.

But no one was more taken aback than George to see Nicholas present at table that afternoon for dinner, even if it was in the middle of the third course, and interpreted his sudden advent as a favourable omen that all past grievances were forgiven and forgot. Nicholas, not one to carry a grudge to extreme, saw no reason to disillusion George on this score as time was growing more precious by the hour and there was, after all, nought to be gained by prolonging hostilities. Quentin was due to return in little over two months to find them in a worse predicament than before, and even if he had, by some odd quirk of fate, undergone a change of heart during his absence, it would of a surety revert to its original when he discovered they had pledged his new ruby and gold-hilted dress sword, ivory and gold toothpick case, and silver-mounted duelling pistols to the meanest penny-pincher in town.

With such a cloud of doom suspended over their heads it was not surprising that neither could command much appetite, and while George sat stabbing at a solitary olive which continuously eluded his fork, his hang-dog visage killing any attempt at conversation, Nicholas rallied courage to defy him.

"Ahem, han't got long, y' know, George," he saw fit to point out anon, inhaling a pinch of snuff with the nicety born of much practice.

"Two months, nineteen days to be exact!" snapped George, loth to be reminded.

"Er—what d'ye plan doin' now? Got t' do somethin', gad! Can't just sit here—"

"Then *you* think of something! You forget, going up to London was my idea, and look what a Pandora's box that turned out to be."

"M-Me? Demn it, George, ye know I'm no good at that sort o' thing. Too shallow brained. Ye've always been the clever one, George," wheedled Nicholas as only he knew how. "Even Quen's said so."

Pride oozed over George at this unexpected praise.

"Nonetheless, Nicky," he sighed, gazing nostalgically round the huge dining-room, which was hung and upholstered with yellow damask, reflecting the afternoon sunshine about them like a halo. "Whatever chances, we shan't be living here for very much longer."

"Fie on ye, George, for the mopish log y' are," rebuked Nicholas, shaking out his napkin and sending clouds of snuff airborne. "Cheer up, man! There's boun' t' be the convent'nal betrothal period o' some months, arrangements t' be made—"

"Humph! You think Quen will follow convention?"

"Been ponderin', George. Might well be Matilda Foreshaw. Stap me, if she didn't eye Quen throughout the entire evenin' at the Duchess o' Queensberry's rout.

Dogged his heels, she did, where'er he went, and to put a crown on't—"

"It don't signify," groused George. "I can't see Quen shackling himself to such an one, I'm not sorry to say."

"But damme, George, she's not a female t' be gainsaid! Ecod, a determined wench if e'er I saw one! A force t' be reckoned with."

"And so is Quen," countered George, irritably. "The question is not who, but when."

"Natheless, George, ye must concede 'tis dev'lish strange," pursued Nicholas, bubbling with curiosity. "Rot me, 'tan't Christian t' envelope y'r future bride in a fog o' secrecy. It don't bear thinkin' what his acquaintance will say when he suddenly produces his Countess at Court like somethin' fished out o' the Grand Canal in the dead o' night."

"Foreign?" choked George. "Y-You think she'll be a f-foreigner?"

"Sure t'be, George. Ain't Quen fetchin' her home with him from the Tour? 'Sides which, 'tan't the thing for English ladies o' refinement. 'Od's life, instant death t' the complexion!"

Apparently the possibility that his future sister-in-law might not be of English extraction had never occurred to George.

"Demmed strange," went on Nicholas, unwittingly creasing his smooth forehead in contemplation. "Not like Quentin t' treat such vital matter so flippant, sink me if 'tis."

"And while we waste time debating it, Quen himself will be marching through the door with the female in question before we've done planning what we're about!" remonstrated George, thudding down his glass, which miraculously remained intact.

" 'Pon honour, 'twould almost seem as if he were loth to put her on show," continued Nicholas unperturbed, to sit bolt upright of a-sudden. "I-I say, George, y-ye don't think 'tis like t' be Catherine Dalrymple?"

"Fustian! I collided with her only last Thursday noon, tripping gaily in the Mall and clutching at my Lord Pembroke's arm like one possessed."

"Pembroke, egad! M' lady hazards her reputation."

"In any event," retorted George, growing more irritable, "she's the last female in Christendom to take pity on us and ransom us from the Fleet! Animate your brain, man! Think!"

Nicholas scowled petulantly across the decanters and silver plate at George.

" 'Odsbobs! How d'ye expect me to command brains when you've got 'em all?"

George's thick dark brows united across his nose like storm clouds gathering over a mountain peak.

"S-Sorry, George," faltered Nicholas, to brighten immediately. "Gad! What a splendid idea!"

"What is?"

"Quen's future bride, she might be quite wealthy. And if she's a female o' gen'rous heart could take pity on us and—"

"Huh! As much pity as Quen will allow."

"But what female o' distinguished family would wish t' boast two brothers-in-law in the debtors' cell? Think o' the scandal!"

"Caro Prentiss would," replied George bluntly. "Her cousin Benjamin gasped his last in King's Bench Prison, so rumour has it."

A peculiar asphyxiating sound erupted from Nicholas.

"M-Methinks of a sudden that marriage might prove the lesser o' the evils."

George felt obliged to agree. Throughout the tense hours at the gaming tables this gruesome prospect had reared its head at disconcerting intervals until his final run of devastating luck when he had acknowledged it inevitable. Therefore, he was now reluctantly prepared to devote serious consideration to the Earl's suggestion, ludicrous though it had seemed at the time.

This, George endeavoured to convey to Nicholas.

"I've been giving some thought to the wretched business, Nicky, and decided . . . hum . . ."

"Well? What have ye decided, damme?"

George was not quite sure, and found putting it into words even more complicated.

"If you remember, Nicky, Quen suggested we both wed heiresses."

"Yes! Yes! And?"

"I don't believe we need to."

"Ye don't?" Nicholas bobbed up agog and moved five places nearer to his brother lest the flunkeys should chance to overhear what he anticipated was to be extremely confidential.

"No—er—not both of us, that is," appended George, taking an unprecedented interest in the number of enamel buttons adorning his multi-coloured velvet waistcoat.

"Ye mean, one of us is t' wed, and one isn't?" queried Nicky suspiciously, dubious ramblings circulating deep within. "Don't relish the sound o' this above half, egad!"

"Don't be a snivelling coward, Nicky!" reprimanded his brother contemptuously. "You must surely agree that there's no point in both of us sealing our nuptial doom!"

"Aye, I'll say amen t' that, George."

"And the other is going to have just as awkward a time of it finding a beast—er—beaùtiful heiress the other will want to marry, isn't he?"

"Hm, if ye say so, George."

"Good, then it's all settled!"

"What's settled? Damme, I lost ye somewhere betwixt the nuptial doom and the heiress! P'raps ye'd clarify, brother, who's t' do the choosin' and who the weddin'?"

George halted three feet from the doors, cursing under his breath at Nicholas being unusually perceptive on this particular day.

"Good heavens, Nicky! It's obvious!" he rounded on the sceptical Nicholas. "Look at me! Who would want to gaze upon a visage like mine across the breakfast table for the rest of their days? So, *you* must wed the girl when I have found her."

Nicky's alabaster complexion suddenly out-reddened his crimson frock-coat and his lower jaw wagged helplessly up and down in a vain effort to make intelligible speech. He eventually met with success.

"I'll be damned in perdition if I will!" he vituperated.

"And you'll be damned in the Fleet if you don't!" countered George blisteringly.

"A pox on ye! I shan't wed anyone at your biddin'! I'm promised to Petronella Wilchards and I'll wed none other! Gad, I'd as lief suffer transportation! No! No! Shan't! Never!" he ranted, pacing wildly round the room, his eyes flashing, flaming, at George. "Damme! D'ye realise this sublime creature actually stooped t' offer herself? To *me?* She's mine, mine! And no one, no one, I tell ye, is wrestin' her from me grasp!"

"No one's trying to wrest her from your grasp!" bellowed George, pounding the table to the jangle and tinkle of china and glass. "You can keep the accursed female! But you aren't obliged to wed her!"

For one terrible moment it seemed that Nicholas might burst into flames.

"What the devil d'ye mean b' that?" he challenged, thumping the table, just as soundly. "Burn an' blister me, were ye not me own brother, me own kith an' kin, I'd slap the insolence of y'r ugly phiz and have ye on the lawn at dawn! Nay, this instant!"

"Be sensible, Nicky," placated George, though unwittingly goading his brother the more. "Content yourself with being her lover—er—when she's wed, of course. Hang me, how can you even consider marrying in all honour a wench in her position without a brass farthing to your name? B' gad, she has looks I grant you, and wealth, but not sufficient to cover our debts—even should her father countenance your suit."

"I will wed her! I will!" cried Nicholas in fury, a lock of hair dangling down his outraged face. "I care not if her father cuts her off with the proverbial shilling, devil take 'im, I'll still wed her even if we're forced t' elope! And neither you nor Quentin—aye, Sir Jason Wilchards, t' boot—is goin' t' stop me! So ye can sharpen y'r wits on that, brother!"

"But you've got all the attributes, dammit!"

"And you've got no attachments, lastin' or otherwise!"

Tense silence fell all around as each stood, their eyes cauterising each other until George relinquished the battle with a shrug and sat down again.

"All this wrangling is getting us no further forward," he rasped, lapsing into concentrated thought.

"Draw lots. Y're fond o' gamin'. Why not try the cards, or the dice?"

"No, I have a better idea," proposed George, the nearest he had been to actually smiling since he had won the thirty thousand guineas, as a gleam sprang to his eyes. "We'll obey Quentin's command! We'll find an heiress and—"

"Ha! And where d' ye expect to find one, eh? Hanging on yonder elm?"

"—and let her choose between us," completed George, ignoring the interruption. "Whoever she chooses must marry her without question and pay the other's debts. Are we agreed?"

"Hanged if we are!" objected Nicholas as before. "She's boun' t' choose me!"

"Don't be so certain," flung back George. "She could well be enamoured of large noses, even have one herself. After all, it's her fortune we want. There's no guarantee she'll outshine the Gunnings."

Following this assurance Nicholas reluctantly agreed, though nurturing every intention of presenting himself in the worst possible manner to the female in question, so much so, that she would seize George to her bosom thus leaving himself free to wed his fair Petronella.

"Er—s'posin' she refuses t' wed either of us?"

"Then we'll continue with our quest until we find one that will," pointed out George, impatiently. "It shouldn't take long as the season's drawing to a close and the cream of society will be homeward bound to the country—"

"Well, what's that to do with anythin'?"

George cursed under his breath. "Dammit, Nicky!

Have you forgotten how lonely and treacherous the roads out of London can be?" he clarified with a nudge and a wink.

Nicholas gave a squawk of alarm. "Y-Ye don't mean t' waylay an' rob 'em o' their jewels, George, l-like common f-felons?"

"Not their infernal gew-gaws, blockhead! Their eligible daughters!"

This was even worse!

"Y-Ye mean ki-kidnappin'? H-Holdin' 'em t' ransom? Gad! Ye've blown y'r wits, George! 'Tis veritable law-breakin'! Forsooth, I'll ha' no part 't!"

"Control yourself, brother. I did not mean kidnapping in the accepted sense of the word! I meant simply that we would bring her here, present her with our proposal of marriage in all honour, and if she sees fit to reject it, we'll send her on her way and try another, without ill-feeling on either side."

"Ye promise? 'Pon oath?"

George so promised and the suggestion met with Nicky's dubious approval.

Four

───◆◆◆───

Although the popularity of the little seaside town of Brighthelmstone was merely in its embryo, the craze for sea-bathing generated by the eminent Doctor Richard Russell had already begun, and as the village of Carnleigh enjoyed the privileged position of being directly *en route* from the Capital to the resort it boasted tolerable renown. It also boasted an attraction for anyone wielding palette and brush to come and perch upon the rustic bridge spanning its gurgling stream and capture for posterity the neatly arrayed thatched cottages and quaint historic taverns.

Thus, Carnleigh was honoured by frequent visitors, many of great consequence who stood in need of some establishment to pander to their fastidious tastes. An assortment of inns had sprung up for this reason but none to equal the post-house bearing the name of The King Charles—who was majestically portrayed upon the signs suspended at intervals around the half timbered walls. The inn's forty-six rooms were put to excellent use by the influx of travellers at the season's end to such a degree that many slept upon the floor whilst servants were accommodated in the barn close by.

It was to bide outside this notable hostelry upon

such an occasion that George and Nicholas came with coach and four in search of their heiress, choosing the subtle shades of night to cloak their dubious deeds from view. Upon arrival George insisted the vehicle remain unseen yet conveniently positioned to effect a swift departure should the need arise. This accomplished, he then adjured Nicholas to sit quietly within the coach and await his return whilst he went off to survey the scene.

The coachyard was well illuminated by the lights from the inn and sundry carriages and Nicholas peered out until George had disappeared amongst the crowd of fine ladies, gentlemen, footmen, ostlers and wenches, when he sat back to gaze disconsolately round himself, wondering what manner of trouble his brother was about to embroil him in this time. To say he was extremely ill at ease would be no exaggeration, for George seemed rather reluctant to divulge the more intricate details of his plan which invariably meant that he, and not George, would end up suffering the consequences. Upon reflection, there was not a single occasion he could call to mind when—

"Pardon me, good sir," a cultured feminine voice intruded upon his meditations, bringing him up with a jolt to gape incredulously down through the doorway at the neatly attired, comely owner of the voice as if he had never clapped eyes upon a female before, "but is this equipage perchance for hire?"

Nicholas recovered the instant his eye alighted upon the gems flashing in her ears and about her elegant neck.

" 'S life, ma'am," he replied eagerly, bounding from the coach with astounding alacrity, casting George's explicit commands to the winds. "I dare say it could be arranged. Er—permit me t' present m'self, I am the Honourable Nicholas Shadwick, o' Carnleigh Hall over yonder, and prodigiously at y'r service," announced he magniloquently, sweeping his feet with his plumed beaver in his most elaborate bow to further ingratiate himself.

The young female, however, would seem just as anxious to impress.

"Carnleigh Hall! N-Not the seat of the much acclaimed Earl of Carnleigh?" gasped she with admirable conviction, as if she had not already perceived the Carnleigh coat-of-arms emblazoned on the coach panels, which could scarcely be ignored.

Nicholas puffed out his chest. "The same, ma'am. I ha' the honour and privilege to be his lordship's brother and next in line to the title—er—after George, that is," he appended, inaudibly.

"Well, I do declare! What dost thou say to that, Amelia?" she called under her right arm to Nicky's astonishment for there was nought to indicate that anyone else was present. "This kind gentleman is the brother of a noble lord no less."

It was here that Nicky's gaze alighted upon a small figure huddled beneath the damsel's cloak as if sheltering from the elements of mid-winter rather than a balmy eve in mid-June.

"My cousin, sir, Miss Amelia Reynolds," she informed him politely, urging her diffident cousin of some seventeen summers to make her curtsy to the gentleman before she herself followed suit, pronouncing her name to be, "Miss Diane Winstone, sir, pleased to make your acquaintance. Had I but known you belonged to one of the most distinguished families in the land," she went on, offering up a silent prayer for this blatant untruth, "I vow I should ne'er have approached you in such indelicate fashion."

"I beg ye, Miss Winstone, ma'am," quoth Nicholas, almost prostrating himself with condescension as the gems sparkled and danced before his avid gaze. "Repine no more on't! Me coach and four are at y'r disposal, an ye so wish't."

"Indeed, sir, we do have most urgent need of some conveyance to support us to the next inn, for this one, as you see, is already quite crowded out. And alas, my cousin here is failing fast—"

"She is ill?" broke in Nicholas with concern.

"I-I know not, sir, but she certainly suffers acute exhaustion and trembles violently in spasms, as if with ague! And see how wan she is," she invited, folding back the capacious hood of her young cousin's capuchin to reveal a ringlet-framed elfin face which did assuredly assume to deathly hue in the coach lights.

The opportunity was too good to be ignored! It was heaven sent! George would be pleased, thrilled Nicholas who, without more ado, hailed his postilion from the box to help him assist the ladies inside and hoist their baggage on top.

"Say no more, ma'am. Pray step up," requested Nicholas, offering his arm.

And between himself and Miss Winstone the sickly Miss Reynolds was ably assisted into the coach to have her knees enveloped in a thick travelling rug, and her cousin seated beside her with a comforting arm about her shoulders, while Nicholas occupied a seat opposite.

"If I mayst make s' bold, Miss Winstone," he overtured discreetly, upon observing the lady more clearly inside the vehicle. "Ye seem t' be a trifle—er—exhausted y'rself."

"La, I must own, Mr. Shadwick," sighed she wearily, sinking back into the luxurious upholstery, "that I was about to relinquish all hope until I spied your carriage. And I swear it was sheer desperation which prompted me to accost you as I did for, in truth, I felt quite on the verge of collapse."

As if immediately regretting confiding so much to this utter stranger who could conceivably seek to take advantage of her defenceless condition, she strove to give the lie to her words by suddenly sitting bolt upright, blinking her heavy-rimmed eyes into full awareness.

Howbeit, although the Honourable Nicholas had earned a considerable reputation with the fair sex since his first conquest at the tender age of five years, this time all thought of seduction—even had his heart not already been in Petronella's keeping—was obliterated by the overwhelming knowledge that within ten minutes of his arrival at The King Charles Inn he was on his way home with, not one heiress which would have been miraculous enough, but two! George could not fail to be proud of him! Success now lay in their grasp! Their tribulations were at an end, for it was scarce likely that both young ladies would cherish aversions to large noses—especially Miss Reynolds who was rather plain, though she did have the most fetching *retroussé* nose Nicholas had ever seen. The only problem was that she was a little too young and therefore possibly unable to control George with the firm hand he needed. Now Miss Winstone, on the other hand, could be accredited quite a beauty—even on his own fastidious standards.

For the second time his experienced eye traversed her face and form—as far as he could beneath the cloak—unable to find a single flaw in her complexion, huge velvety brown eyes, dimpled if perverse chin, nut-brown curls, and even her shapely ankle of which he had been accorded a glimpse as she had ascended the coach steps. In fact, the only adverse criticism Nicholas had to make was upon the lady's attire which was a trifle démodé, though of admirable quality, nonetheless, and flattering to her features. Obviously Miss Winstone dressed thus by desire rather than necessity, decided he finally, for her pearls and diamonds seemed genuine enough and she certainly had the air of one of consequence, as if accustomed to delegating orders.

However, if he nurtured any doubts about the young ladies' station in life they were instantly dispelled by Miss Reynolds who, contrary to her cousin, was dressed in the height of fashion from what he could again detect 'neath the cloak, which alone was bedecked with costly gold lace and of Parisian origin. Not to mention her gold embroidered slipper protruding from under a gown of flounced satin and the diamond pins securing her black hair. Yes, Miss Amelia Reynolds was unmistakably a young lady of affluence, and accustomed to having her every whim indulged if the petulant lower lip was aught to go by.

These particulars Nicholas perceived in a flash whilst Miss Winstone drew breath to resume her discourse.

"I am escorting my young cousin to her great-aunt's home in Berkshire where we are to sojourn a while, as her parents—my aunt and uncle—have been called away up to Scotland to visit a sick relative."

"May I presume to question exactly where in Berkshire y'r destined for, ma'am?" queried Nicholas, the essence of gentlemanly politeness.

"Certainly, Mr. Shadwick. It is—er" she tailed off to

fumble beneath her cloak in her under-pocket, her gloved hand at length emerging clutching a piece of well-fingered paper which she unfolded as best she could with her one free hand, to enunciate: "Thatcham! Three miles out of Newbury on the road to Bath."

"Thatcham? And ye travel from whence, ma'am?"

"Why London, of course."

"London!" echoed Nicholas, struggling to suppress the elation in his voice, for this gave every indication that the young ladies were well and truly lost, which would place them at even greater disadvantage and wholly at his mercy.

"Is something amiss, Mr. Shadwick?" questioned Diane, naively. "You appear to be surprised."

"Dammit, ma'am—er—y'r pardon, I-I mean, fie on't, but y're headed due south," spluttered Nicholas.

"South? Does that mean we won't see Thatcham tonight?"

"Nay, nor any other, Miss Winstone, unless ye undertake a major detour."

"Oh dear," she lamented forlornly. "Where can we have gone astray?" Then more to herself, "It must surely have been when that beastly axle broke on our carriage and we were obliged to hire a post-chaise." She tut-tutted in annoyance. "The servants will probably be there by now and wondering what on earth has befallen us."

At this, Amelia raised her weary head to focus her hollow eyes upon her cousin, her lower lip trembling visibly as if tears were imminent.

"Sh-Shant's we s-see Aunt D-Dalby soon?" she whimpered, a tear already coursing down her face.

"Of course we shall, my love," cooed Diane, caressing the child's pallid cheek. "I do assure you, if you close your eyes and go to sleep we will be at Aunt Dalby's before you open them again."

Nicholas realised the absurdity of this but deemed it circumspect to hold his peace as Amelia's head drooped back onto her cousin's comforting shoulder in utter contentment.

"In truth, I beg ye, Miss Winstone," besought Nicholas in a vital whisper. "Despair not! All will come about, I swear on oath! Ye may trust me implicitly for the gentleman I am."

It was precisely this that now troubled Miss Winstone, though she gave no intimation of it. True, the Earl of Carnleigh was reputed to be a gentleman of honour but that did not guarantee the brother would be bound to follow suit. And if the dubious way he continually eyed her was aught to go by it would seem that her suspicions were not without foundation.

Diane Winstone, of good pedigree though an orphan for the past five years, was well-accustomed to taking care of herself and was certainly not the type of female to calmly accept life's adversities without doing something to avert them. Indeed, not only was she resourceful but uncommonly astute, which would never have occurred to Nicholas who found it impossible to comprehend how anyone travelling to Newbury and finishing up *en route* to Brighthelmstone could boast this quality in any degree. Suffice it to say, then, that our Miss Winstone held this perception in abeyance until danger threatened when she did not hesitate to draw upon it in commensurate measure. For this reason, unbeknownst to Nicholas, she had assumed custody of her cousin's most valuable trinkets, for no highwayman would surely have the audacity to molest her person!

The lady's former suspicions graduated to undeniable fact at this point when the coach glided to a standstill at the grand entrance of a huge establishment, for it was quite evident—though darkness limited her vision—that whatever it was, it certainly was not an inn. As there was nought to be achieved at this stage by protesting about she knew not quite what, and she was loth to risk disquieting her charge any more than was absolutely necessary (who would no doubt be disquieted enough to discover their destination not Aunt Dalby's as anticipated), she alighted from the carriage with dignity, though of a frigid sort, inviting her cousin to do likewise, and then hustled her up the steps of the intimidating Doric portico and into the palatial hall of the Carnleighs before Amelia had time to open her sleepy eyes to the true situation.

Although the hall boasted the welcoming bright lights of three ponderous chandeliers and an inviting staircase of white marble and gold, spread with a gaily patterned Persian carpet, Diane felt Amelia give an involuntary shiver which she had to own was justified when she raised her eyes to the great dome way above them, then down the niched walls where sculptured gods and nymphs stood housed, displaying their abundant charms to the household, and on down to the mosaic tiled floor.

Shielding her cousin's innocent gaze with a discreet hand from the blatant exhibition of the human body, Diane hastened after a powdered flunkey who conducted them across the hall and into the Small Drawingroom. Here, the decor was much more to her taste with cream brocade hangings and upholstery, red velvet curtains at the towering windows, and matching carpet upon the floor, all of which pervaded her with an element of pleasant relief.

Nicholas was not long to follow on her heels, and having divested himself of his outdoor apparel, invited the young ladies to do the same, at which Diane was heard to demur most strongly.

"Mr. Shadwick," she questioned in chilling tones, "would you be good enough to tell us where we are?"—though it seemed perfectly obvious.

Nicholas lingered by the door, nervously gnawing his bottom lip and transferring his weight from one foot to the other. Now that he stood confronting the ladies in the precincts of his brother's house the idea of abducting them and his marriage proposition seemed the height of the ridiculous.

"Well, sir," she prompted, striving to suppress her indignation, which was mounting visibly. "Surely you do not expect me to believe this the tap-room of some tavern?"

He took three brave steps forward, had second thoughts, took one back and cleared his throat.

"Er—n-no, ma'am."

"Indeed, sir! An I much mistake it, 'tis the home of your brother the Earl, is it not?"

"Er—y-yes, ma'am," responded Nicholas like a rebuked schoolboy, unable to meet the lady's piercing eye. "P-Pray don't alarm y'rself, Miss Winstone. Me brother's abroad on the Tour at present, and an't expected t' return for another month, so ye've nought t' fear."

"That is a matter of opinion, Mr. Shadwick," she retorted tartly. "Surely you do not have the effrontery to expect me to believe that this exceedingly accommodating arrangement was not deliberately contrived?"

"By the death, ma'am!" protested Nicholas, tugging furiously at his strangulating stock. " 'Tis pos-'tively insultin', damme! Ye do me grave injustice! Egad, y're not the only one whose honour's on the choppin' block. 'Tis like me brother may return earlier than antic'-pated . . ."

To Nicky's relief his interrogator's attention was waylaid suddenly by her charge who, having been dumbfounded with awe at her surroundings, now recovered her speech, along with her disappointment that she was not, after all, at her dear Aunt Dalby's as she had been led to expect.

"This isn't Aunt Dalby's parlour, Di," she wailed plaintively, gazing round the sumptuous furnishings, and wondering how she had found them so inspiring. "Wh-Where are we?. . .I don't like it. . .I-I'm afraid . . . I want Aunt Dalby—"

"Sh-Sh, my dear one. And so you shall have your aunt as soon as may be."

"But you said when I opened my eyes again she would be there, Di, and she's not! You promised!"

"Yes, I know I did, Amelia," sighed Diane, even more fatigued than her cousin which the situation did nought to alleviate. "But we somehow lost our way and this kind gentleman has come to our aid." She fixed Nicholas with a poignant eye, challenging him to defy her in this.

"W-We are to shelter here? Stay the night?"

"If Mr. Shadwick would be so magnanimous as to accommodate us," she replied hesitantly, glancing appealingly at Nicholas, such a pathetic appeal that he readily acknowledged her a veritable witch! A female Garrick who changed her mood as a chameleon did its skin. Heaven preserve whoe'er took such an one to wife!

"Forsooth, Miss Winstone," gushed Nicholas, falling

over himself to oblige the lady, though he knew not why, "rooms are already prepared, and y'r baggage disposed therein. T' offer ye sanctuary for the night was all I intended from the outset, my life on't," he vowed fervently, distorting the truth slightly. "Ask George, I'll warrant he'll verify it!"

"George? And pray who is George?"

"Er—m' brother, second eldest,—hum—in direct line to the title, dammim," muttered Nicholas.

"May I ask how many brothers you have, Mr. Shadwick?" queried she with misgiving.

"Just Quentin, head o' the house," he supplied obligingly. "Then George just mentioned who—"

"Yes, then yourself?" urged she on a note of impatience, loth to envisage spending the night beneath the same roof as half the male population of Carnleigh.

"Aye, me after George, and—hem—second in line to inherit."

"That is all?" Miss Winstone seemed visibly relieved. "And George?" probed she, hopefully. "He is away from home too, perhaps?"

"No, not George! George should be here s-some . . . where . . . George?" pondered Nicholas in sudden perplexity. "What the deuce became of him? Last I remember—"

Here the door unexpectedly flew open and clashed back against the wall causing considerable vibration to everything in the room, including Nicholas and his female companions.

"Er—would this be George?" asked Miss Winstone calmly of Nicholas, who could do nought but gape at the wild apparition in the doorway.

How anyone could be relied upon to determine the identity of the intruder was incomprehensible for it was quite beyond the naked eye to penetrate the grime, filth and much else of road, field and hedgerow, to detect if what lay beneath were human or no.

" 'S life, ma'am, I-I'm not quite . . . sure . . ." responded Nicholas, sidling gingerly forward the better to view the strange phenomenon. "G-George? Is't you?"

"Of course it's me, you thundering oaf!" barked the unmistakable voice of George. "I'd scarce be standing here if I were Dobson's scarecrow!"

"But, ecod, what's happened t' ye?"

"Would you look any better, brother, if you'd fallen into ditches, tangled with thickets, and ended feet-uppermost in a pig-sty?" rasped George, ignoring the company as he groped about his sodden person for his handkerchief, nurturing a forlorn hope that it might still be dry, when a footman ran to his aid with a napkin. "Well might I ask what happened to *you*, brother Nicholas? When I returned you'd vanished without trace, leaving me to foot it home like some common clod-hopper! Dammit, I ought to horsewhip you!"

"I-I'm exceedin' sorry, G-George," whimpered Nicholas, retiring a safe distance as George mopped the grime from his face revealing an expression defying all description. "W-Why didn't ye hire a horse?"

"Because there wasn't one to be had this side of Hayward's Heath!"

"Please, Mr. Shadwick, I beg you will not hold your brother responsible for what has befallen," ventured Diane, lest the bellicose exchange end in blows. "I am the one to be censured as it was I who prevailed upon him to convey my cousin and myself to the next hostelry, for my cousin, as you see, is not at all well, and The King Charles was quite crowded out—as you must have already witnessed."

George turned his smouldering gaze upon the females, his manner mellowing a little as his eye alighted on the pale, thin Amelia languishing upon her cousin's arm—and mellowing even more at sight of the sparkling gems.

"Er—your servant, ma'am. I trust you will forgive my disarray," he bowed stiffly. "I know not from whence you come nor whomsoever you be, but nonetheless, I suggest you conduct your young cousin above-stair without delay. We may resume our discussion at supper."

"I ordered rooms to be prepared, George," burst out Nicholas, anxious to regain his lost favour.

"Good, Nicky! Then perhaps Miss—er—Miss—"

"Winstone, sir, Miss Diane Winstone. And my cousin, Miss Amelia Reynolds," supplied Diane, curtsying with a grateful smile at George's estimable foresight in allowing Amelia to retire before she should collapse in a dead faint at their feet.

Five

Whilst Diane was seeing her cousin comfortably bestowed in her bedchamber, George was in his rooms cleansing away the dirt and disfigurement of the road, closeted with his man, and Nicholas who fawned upon his brother the while, relating all that had happened, laying particular stress upon the obvious affluence of the young ladies and the clever way in which he had managed to abduct two such heiresses quite unaided, for which George might extend a modicum of gratitude.

But George *was* grateful, exceedingly so! And even overtured a pat upon his younger brother's slender shoulder to prove it.

The hour was well advanced when the two sat down, suitably attired, to sup with Miss Winstone—whose own toilette needed nought to be desired, despite her obvious tiredness—and the topic of the young ladies' presence at Carnleigh was tactfully resumed. George, having strategically positioned himself at table not too far from Nicholas, was well-able to exercise the necessary caution to prevent him encroaching upon the holy ground of wealth and wedlock, for he was anxious not to ruin all by a careless word at this crucial stage. Time enough on the morrow to state their proposition when they were all refreshed from a sound sleep and a little better tempered and acquainted.

Nevertheless, time being of the essence, George lost no time the following morning after breaking their fast, deeming conditions as auspicious as they ever would be to put the proposal to Miss Winstone. The offer would undoubtedly have been extended to Miss Reynolds also, had not she expressed an urgent need to keep to her room on account of her poor condition, which seemed to be somewhat worse.

And so the three concerned assembled themselves in the library where the Earl had first made known the dire position to his brothers, seated at his huge desk where George now saw fit to establish himself, as if he had already succeeded to the status of lord and master of the Shadwick household.

Apart from a little apprehension concerning her cousin's state of health, Miss Winstone was surprisingly calm, though understandably puzzled, as she sat directly opposite George, her brunette curls swept becomingly aloft 'neath a white French cap trimmed with pink lace and tied under her dimpled chin with pink ribbons. Her gown, of matching pink taffeta trimmed with furbelows, was worn over an oblong hoop and was certainly impressive, endowing her indeed with an aura of affluence, even if the style was, as the last, a trifle out of fashion. Moreover, her every gesture and expression, portrayed the accomplished society lady, as if she had seen and heard more than her twenty-three years should warrant.

Meanwhile, Nicholas skulked in the background, wishing he might evaporate into the book-shelves yet equally wanting not to miss a single item which might affect him directly, and hoping George would not detect his attempt at subterfuge by deliberately dressing himself down in order to swing the pendulum of Miss Winstone's decision in his, George's, favour. To this end he had selected an out-worn suit of sage superfine, trimmed with lace of a peculiar brown which was, to the discerning eye, nothing more than silver lace in advanced stages of tarnish. His face was quite devoid of paint, powder and other allied artifices, while his beautiful hair was obscured 'neath a grizzled wig. And whereas he had resisted a feverish impulse to rip holes in his beige silk stockings they nevertheless sagged round his legs to his satisfaction. In truth, each brother had taken the necessary pains with his appearance, George to appear as becoming as Nicholas, and Nicholas as unbecoming as George. But as it chanced, the two would have better expended their energies in a rubber or two of whist.

"Miss—er—Winstone," began George with an air of authority, chasing round in his brain to recapture the elusive words of his well rehearsed speech, "I have, that is, my brother and I have a sort of proposition to put before you."

"Proposition, Mr. Shadwick? To me?" queried she, sitting up with interest, more perhaps because the mystery surrounding them all was finally to be expounded, for no one, let alone anyone with Miss Winstone's perception, could have failed to notice the devious whisperings and not-too-surreptitious glances cast her way ever since her arrival.

"As you may have gathered, ma'am," resumed George, making prodigious bother about sharpening a quill to write precisely nothing, "I am not given to flowery speeches. I do not boast a turn of phrase like my—hum—brothers—"

"Ecod, George!" interjected Nicholas. "I think Miss Winstone will ha' gathered that by now."

"So without any ado, I shall simply state the facts, after which I shall make the—hum—proposal which, an you see fit—"

"All right! All right! Damme, George, ye've said y'r piece now get on with it!" goaded Nicholas, anxious to know the outcome and whether he was to live or die.

Again did George control his temper at Nicky's unwarranted interruption which he sensed was purposely designed to provoke a scene in front of the lady in order that she might choose anyone rather than him.

"The position is this, ma'am. We are come upon hard times, and are obliged to seek means whereby we may—er—come about, so to speak," resumed George, warming to his theme. "We are merely unfortunates whose substance has—hum—fallen by the wayside, but would stress that we are nonetheless, ma'am, upright honest gentlemen—" he ignored a gasp of incredulity from Nicky, "—who are down of their luck. You see before you two victims of—"

"Gaming plague!"

"Nicky!"

"S-Sorry, George."

Miss Winstone did not find the drama being enacted for her exclusive benefit in any way entertaining, although it might have been better appreciated had not she been in such haste to be gone on her journey, and could not as yet see how the gentlemen's state of finance, penurious or otherwise, had any direct connection with herself.

"To continue, Miss Winstone, ma'am," George addressed her again, eager not to lose her interest. "We find ourselves out of fortune and threatened, nay, doomed to spend the rest of our days chained up in the debtors' cell, unless we can—hum—avert it."

Diane seemed more confused than before.

"You desire a sum of money? A-A loan, Mr. Shadwick?"

"No, ma'am, an heiress."

"An heiress!"

"A loan is but a temporary measure. Besides, we have no hope of ever being able to repay it."

"But what gives you leave to assume that I am an heiress?" she exclaimed, taken aback.

A suspicious glint sprang to George's eye. "Are you trying to tell us that you are not an heiress, ma'am, when you arrive here bedecked in jewels?"

"Oh! N-No, of course not," she replied doubtfully. "Er—yes, you are right, sirs. I am an heiress."

George and Nicholas exchanged curious glances at this strange admission, but deigned not to comment.

"I fear the remedy to our problem must be more substantial, —er—more permanent—"

"Y You intend to r-rob us?" she pursued, her brown eyes widening.

"No, Miss Winstone."

"K-Keep us here against our will, perhaps? F-For ransom money?"

"Not if the problem can be resolved by alternative means—"

"Gadswoons! Ye can't keep 'em prisoners, George! Ye can't! Ye promised on oath if they refused us ye'd let 'em go!" vituperated Nicholas in support of the ladies, equally anxious for his own skin.

George pounded the desk with his fist to silence his agitated brother.

"If Miss Winstone and her cousin see fit to reject

our proposal, Nicholas, then we will have no choice but to follow this course!"

"B-But what about Quen? Ye gods, man! He'll rend ye apart at the seams when he returns!"

"By which time," countermanded George, "the whole sordid business will be over and done with!"

"Ye can't be certain!" argued Nicholas, growing just as hot under his stock. "Confound it, could take months 'fore her sire coughs up the lucre! Meanwhile Quen will be here with his affianced and we'll be in the Fleet!"

"Not in the presence of the future Countess of Carnleigh! Even Quen wouldn't dare to have us arrested whilst in her company, no matter who she be."

"Forgive me interrupting," ventured Miss Winstone, civilly. "But as it is my fate you are at variance about, may I point out that, anon, you can scarce expect me to remain silent about the whole affair."

"Exactly, ma'am! Ye see, George?" accorded Nicholas, with a cocky toss of his wig. "Miss Winstone an't goin' t' keep quiet."

"And pardon my innate curiosity," went on she, "but am I to understand that your brother, the Earl, is about to wed yet he has not disclosed the name of his betrothed?"

Nicholas nodded his head in confirmation of this. "Though odds are in favour of Matilda Foreshaw," he could not resist apprising her.

"None of which has aught to do with the crucial issue!" snapped George, before turning to address Miss Winstone. "Very well, ma'am, if you refuse to act as our hostage then you must elect to wed one of us."

"Wed you!" ejaculated the lady in astonishment, gazing incredulously from one would-be spouse to the other, until she fell back into her chair and gave licence to a gurgle of laughter.

It was now George and Nicky's turn to look dumbfounded whilst wondering whether to commiserate with or congratulate each other upon their prospective bride's reaction.

"Er—what exactly was it ye said, George?" probed Nicholas.

"I proposed marriage, blast it!" barked George, his wonder yielding to affront, suspecting that yet another ingenious ruse was about to fly through the window.

"Oh, gentlemen!" gasped Miss Winstone, dabbing affectedly at her eyes as she rose from her chair to curtsy in abject apology. "I pray you will excuse my mirth, but when I relate the whole I'm sure you will agree that 'tis all extremely diverting!" And in evidence of this, she indulged in another gurgle of laughter but which she overcame a little quicker than the last.

"Well, ma'am?" snorted George. "We are waiting to be diverted."

Nicholas would have fervently seconded this but he lacked George's forthright approach.

"This ring, good sirs," elucidated the lady, stretching forth her left hand for them to view the diamond and sapphire confection winking and sparkling thereon, "is not simply for adornment."

"Is't not?" queried Nicholas, with the naïveté of a child as he focused his eye enviously upon the flashing gems. "Faith, 'tis a pretty bauble an' no mistake—"

"Oh lud! No! We've been duped! Cozened!" groaned George, clapping hand to head.

"Indeed, gentlemen," agreed Diane with an irresistible smile. "I fancy one could say that you have truly been hoisted upon your own petard."

"Hanged if I understand," declared Nicholas, head shuttling betwixt the two. "What d'ye mean, ma'am? George?"

"It's a betrothal ring, you dunderhead!" shouted George in exasperation. "Which means that our hope of salvation is dashed to pieces! By gad, and that won't be all by a long shot should the lady choose to blab it abroad!"

Nicky's mouth fell ajar. "Y-Y'r betrothed? To wed another?"

"I'm afraid so, Mr. Shadwick," responded she, pleasantly.

"Dammit! Be just our accurst luck to turn out 'tis Quentin she's bespoken by, 's blood! Then there'd be the devil to pay all right!" sounded off George, flinging arms ceilingwards in despair.

"Is there any reason why it shouldn't be?" questioned Miss Winstone, innocently.

The deathly hush was excruciating before George exploded.

"Satan's death! I don't believe it! 'Tis an infernal lie!"

"A-A joke, perhaps?" suggested Nicholas weakly.

"You can't be Quen's future wife! You can't!" cried George, more for his own conviction, for to acknowledge the fact would be to open the flood-gates to disaster. "She's abroad on the Tour with him and they are to return shortly, said so himself!"

"Er—pardon me, George," Nicholas put in with civility. "But Quen said nought I can recall about takin' a future wife away with him. Said he'd bring one back, mind ye, but nought about takin' one there."

"He didn't? You're certain?" probed George, instinctively caressing his neck with misgiving.

"No, George. Remember quite distinctly. Thought she was a deuced Frog, said so y'rself."

"Yes, well, I'm sure Miss Winstone isn't really interested one way or the other about what I thought, Nicky," exclaimed he testily, deciding it high time he set about smoothing out the little difference.

"Simple enough, George," opined Nicholas lackadaisically bethinking he had nought to worry about for it had not been his idea to abduct an heiress. " 'Twould appear that Quentin intended callin' at Thatcham on his return and escortin' Miss Winstone here, eh, ma'am?"

"That is so, Mr. Shadwick."

"But dammit, it-it's incredible!" pursued George unthinking.

"How, sir?" queried the lady indignantly. "Is it so difficult to accept that your brother, the Earl, would choose one such as I to be his future bride?"

"Indeed no, ma'am," exclaimed George, inwardly castigating himself for giving licence to his thoughts, substituting hurriedly: "I-I meant, it was incredible how we should chance upon your—er—self out of all the hundreds of females populating the area at this time of year."

"Ah, yes, Mr. Shadwick," concurred she, smoothing a crease from her gown with a gentle caress. "There I am persuaded to agree with you."

"Just my deuced luck," lamented Nicholas appreciating these odds. "I'd ha' fared better tryin' t' carry off the Queen!"

"Don't bear thinking what Quen 'll say when he finds out what you've done," George saw fit to transfer the blame. "Lud, what a coil! Thank the saints I had no hand in it."

Nicholas rounded on his brother. "Curse ye for a double-dealin' Pharisee! 'Twas y'r own idea from the outset!"

"Mayhap, but I can swear just as truthfully that I was nowhere near the scene of the crime and that I had no knowledge of it," flung back George.

"Please, gentlemen," Miss Winstone interceded to prevent bloodshed. "Do not alarm yourselves. I assure you, I would certainly not have you fight to the death on my account. Imagine what your brother would say upon his return? We will overlook the entire incident and forget that it ever occurred."

"W-We w-will?" stammered the two.

"Never fear that I shall divulge your secret—if you swear not to divulge mine?" she bargained with a coy smile, holding up her beringed finger significantly.

"By the faith, ma'am, that we do swear!" asseverated George. "On our very lives! Don't we, Nicky?"

"Indubitably, George! Ma'am! Most gen'rous o' ye. 'Pon m' soul, I ha' ne'er been so o'ercome wi' gratitude and—"

"Dammit, Nicky, no need to leap overboard," George hissed in the other's ear, before turning benignly to Miss Winstone, doing his level best to ingratiate himself. "It is most kind in you ma'am, to take it all so excellently well. As you say, we will consider the matter closed for it will benefit none to unduly prolong the—hum—painful issue. A coach and six will await you at the door at noon, to transport you to—er—"

"Thatcham, sir," she supplied obligingly.

"Er—Thatcham, as if the incident had never taken place. And moreover, you may rely implacably—"

"Implicitly?"

"Aye, whole-heartedly upon our discretion and when Quentin anon returns with you we will act most convincingly as utter strangers. Won't we, Nicky?"

"Verily, George! No sense in provokin' Quen more than need be."

"None whatsoever, Mr. Shadwick," approved Miss Winstone, proceeding to the door with a whisper of silk petticoats. "Now as the hour advances I must attend my cousin and make arrangements for us to be on our way. You will excuse me?"

"Certainly, ma'am! I do declare that there's not a moment to be lost," enthused George, bowing Miss Winstone out of the door, now every whit as keen to have the lady gone as she was to go. "Burn me, if darkness don't seem to fall 'fore the sun has done setting these days."

"Y'r humble obedient, ma'am," murmured Nicholas as they respectfully, though thankfully, gave a final bow before closing the door upon her retreating person.

Granted, Nicholas and George may have been shocked somewhat by the outcome of the interview, but they would have been shocked even more had they been able to observe their so superior Miss Winstone creeping back to place her delicate pink ear to the library door, to eavesdrop upon their subsequent comments, before tiptoeing softly away, chuckling to herself.

Six

At this stage, a degree of satisfaction was being entertained on both sides; the gentlemen, in the knowledge that they had extricated themselves with admirable finesse from an extremely embarrassing predicament and were to be rid of the lady responsible within the hour, who, furthermore, was to respect their confidence; and Miss Winstone, by the fact that she was escaping from a mad-house with not only her neck and honour intact but her cousin's wealth, also. Not surprisingly, the lady could not quit the house with enough dispatch following the unnerving experience of meeting George and Nicholas for the first time, an unnerving experience by anyone's standards, and desired nothing more than to get to Thatcham where she might regain a modicum of sanity.

It would appear, then, that all had fallen conveniently into place as it ought—but seldom is life so accommodating. Consequently the three concerned had not done thus congratulating themselves upon their fortunate escape when a minor complication arose which was eventually to cause a major disruption in the Shadwick household, namely, young Amelia's delicate condition.

To everyone's alarm and dismay it was discovered

that Miss Reynolds' state of health had declined rather rapidly during the past hour, making it quite impossible for her to travel to Thatcham, or anywhere else. Notwithstanding, hopes were cherished that Amelia would be quite well enough on the morrow to undertake the protracted journey. But alas, next day hopes were again dashed to find the patient even worse, two days after which she developed a raging fever.

At every opportunity George and Nicholas were to be found hovering outside the sickroom, as anxious for their own welfare as they were the patient's, whilst Miss Winstone remained closeted within, ministering to her cousin's needs, adamantly refusing—for some unaccountable reason—to allow anyone else in the room, or to even contact a physician. Day and night she remained by the bed where she slept and partook of her meals. And if she was obliged to quit the room at any time she never failed to lock the door in her wake, almost as if she had some secret concealed therein and was determined that no one should discover it.

It was almost two weeks later at approximately an hour before cock-crow that a ghastly blood-curdling scream suddenly rent the night asunder, causing the entire Shadwick household to start from their beds in terror and bewilderment, and scatter in all directions, trying to ascertain through sleepy eyes and befuddled heads, from whence the sound had come. All seemed agreed upon the west wing when it came again, more unearthly than before, and from—without any doubt—the apartments of Nicholas.

The valet was first to reach his master, closely followed by George whose chambers were in the same wing. Both servant and brother were aghast to find, in the light of a solitary candle, Nicholas seized by violent trembling, in a kind of fit.

He was sitting erect, bedecked in nightcap and shirt in the huge four-poster, pointing wildly with one shaking hand at the looking-glass he held petrified in the other, his eyes protruding from his head in dire fright.

"I've got it! I've got it! I'm doomed! Done for!" he was shrieking frenziedly, as if nothing in the world would pacify him. "Look! Look! Despite me salves and potions! 'Ods death! Me life's finished—"

"Nicky, what the devil is it? Pull yourself together, man!" cried George in alarm, dashing up to the bed and seizing his distraught brother by the shoulders to shake him out of his hysteria, bethinking it nought more serious than a bad dream—to spring back of a sudden, blenching in horror at sight of Nicky's face.

"Saints in heaven!" he swore aloud, then to the valet: "Close the door, Blakeson! And let no one enter on pain of dismissal, you understand? Er—on second thoughts you'd better lock it, I'll need your help. Nicky! What on earth is it?" he demanded, turning back to view Nicholas through strained eyes. "Can't quite make it out in this damned light. More candles, Blakeson!"

"Th-The pox, damn ye! It-It's the small-pox! Can't ye see?"

Although George was harbouring vague suspicions of this the news still came as a considerable blow, and a blistering oath escaped him as Blakeson dutifully approached, bearing two candelabra to illuminate the macabre scene. Indeed, he was forced to agree that things looked bad for Nicky who, in spite of the excruciating evidence in his glass, sat gazing up at George, his every hope hanging upon his brother's assurance that the affliction was not, after all, that accursed malady which had scourged all Europe, killing millions, and which the entire world lived in daily dread of, but in no greater dread than he himself, so fastidious about his looks. And when no such assurance was forthcoming, Nicholas abandoned all hope and lost his head completely.

"Laudanum, Blakeson! Quickly!" commanded George, narrowly evading Nicky's mirror as it flew past his head to shatter against the tapestried wall.

Meanwhile, as the valet searched agitatedly through his master's collection of phials, bottles and jars for the sedative, the noise outside the locked door swelled to deafening proportions as servants from the highest to the lowest gathered to find out what was amiss, headed by none other than Miss Winstone herself who, upon receiving no response to her knocking, kindly volunteered her services through the keyhole.

Before long, Nicky's fair head fell limply onto George's arm and he was laid back upon the feather pillows to rest, while George choked back the anguish welling within him crying out to be released and, assured that his brother was comfortably sleeping, drew the valet aside.

"You understand what this is, Blakeson?" he questioned in a low tone, thankful that the turbulence at the door was abating, but in no state of mind to reason why.

"I-I suspect, sir," acknowledged the valet, bowing with servility.

"And it doesn't alarm you?"

"No, Master George. You see, sir, I was a victim of it myself some years ago, but somehow survived."

"Yet you bear no scar . . ."

"No, sir. I was luckier than most."

George eyed the servant closely, as if meeting him for the first time, unable to fathom this unique breed of man who filled him with a gnawing guilt yet a sense of profound admiration.

"You're a good man, Blakeson," George commended him, hoarsely, a hand venturing to the menial's shoulder in evidence of his deeply disturbed emotions. "My brother is fortunate in his choice . . . Y-You will stay with him? I have much to attend to."

"Master George! Indeed, I'd sacrifice my life for young Master Nicholas! Th-There is no n-need to ask." The valet's voice broke suddenly, despite his twenty years of rigid self-discipline, as he bowed George to the door, where, with a final glance towards the bed, George straightened his betasselled nightcap, wrapped his quilted robe more securely about him, and took his leave.

Upon emerging from the room he was mildly surprised to find only the housekeeper, head-footman and Miss Winstone waiting anxiously. However, it was the unexpected sight of the latter which sent his blood surging furiously through his veins, striking him with the full import of the terrible tragedy which her presence in the house had wrought. To think that Nicky, the brother he loved more than any being on God's earth, though he never would have confessed it, had been cut down by this—this—person! Granted, it was not entirely Miss Winstone's fault that she came to be at Carnleigh at all, but this George chose to overlook in his agony of soul, a feeling wholly alien to him which he knew not how to deal with. He was being driven by some unknown force to find something tangible to blame which would ease his dire suffering, a scapegoat, the role of which Miss Winstone fitted to perfection.

"Madam!" spat he mordaciously. "I would have speech with you belowstairs!"

And with that he stormed off through the catenation of galleries, the heels of his embroidered slippers echoing martially upon the polished floor, leaving her to follow at her own pace.

Diane was about to demur but the dangerous mood of Mr. George Shadwick coupled with the warning looks directed at her from the housekeeper and footman urged her to reconsider and, at length, hasten in his wake. She finally ran him to earth in the Small Drawing-room where he was pacing the floor in acute agitation, wholly ignoring her entrance.

Appreciating the futility in awaiting an invitation to do so, Miss Winstone quietly disposed herself in a high-backed chair close by as George marched to a standstill at a table directly opposite her, gripping its edge until his knuckles glowed white in open contrast to his face which was black with rage. For several seconds he remained thus glowering down at her, breathing heavily, his eyes like balls of fire burning into her being.

Diane fought to meet his gaze, shuffling uneasily in her chair and beginning to suspect he held some personal grievance towards her, perhaps, connected with what had just occurred in Nicholas's bedchamber.

"Miss Winstone!" he bellowed suddenly making her jump. "I care not what state your cousin's health is in, you will pack your bags and clear out of this house immediately!"

She stared back at him, stunned. "I-I beg your pardon?" she stammered, eventually. "D-Did I hear you correctly, sir? You wish us to leave? Tonight? *Now?*"

"Not wish it, ma'am, command it!" stormed he. "You will be gone from here within the hour or else I will have you both forcibly ejected whether you be future sister-in-law or mother-in-law! Is that clear?"

"Perfectly clear, Mr. Shadwick!" retorted she, vehemently, her own feathers now prickling at such unreasonable abuse. "May I enquire the reason behind this sudden burst of hostility?"

"How-How dare you, ma'am!" exploded George anew, giving fullest licence to his inherent aggression. "How dare you sit there and play the innocent after bringing such a vile curse upon my brother!"

"Innocent! I assure you, Mr. Shadwick, I have little choice but to be anything else when I know not what you are rampaging about!"

"You don't, eh?" he rounded on her from the table. "You keep your cousin mysteriously locked away in her room, allowing no one to attend her but yourself lest your secret be discovered, and expect me to—"

"I swear on my cousin's very life, sir, that I have no such secret!" retaliated Diane, her anger and resentment vying with his. "If you will accompany me to my cousin's room now, this very instant you will see that she is over the worst of her sickness. The fever has quite gone and in a day or two the pox will begin to disappear—"

"Aha!" George seized upon the fatal word like a cat on a mouse. "The pox! Condemned from your own lips!"

"There is more than one variety of pox, Mr. Shadwick, as I'm sure you are already agreed—"

"Indeed, ma'am," accorded he with scorn. "But no

doubt you will claim your cousin's to be of the mildest strain?"

"No, not the mildest, sir, but certainly no threat to life nor looks."

"And you expect me to believe this?"

"As you please," replied she brusquely, rising from the chair. "It is painfully obvious that you will not be convinced until you witness it for yourself. If you will be so good as to follow me?"

It was now George's turn to follow humiliatingly in the wake of Miss Winstone, though with some resolution in his stride that he should prove the lady wrong, yet cherishing more than a flicker of hope in his heart that she might after all be right and Nicholas not fallen victim to such an execrable fate.

Upon reaching Amelia's chamber Diane halted at the door to listen awhile, and assured that all was well within, turned to entreat her sceptical companion to be as quiet as possible lest they awaken her sleeping cousin. George acknowledged this with a curt jerk of his head and the two entered, tiptoeing across to stand upon the right of the bed where Diane gently drew back the curtains of both window and bed to allow the grey light of dawn to filter through on to Amelia who lay prone in the lap of Morpheus with arms flung wide and her face clearly exposed for both to see.

"Well, Mr. Shadwick?" prompted Diane, relieved to find her cousin sleeping so tranquilly but wishing that the blisters were a little less obtrusive. "Do not you see how my cousin rests quietly, without any sign of fever whatsoever?"

Howbeit, Diane need not have suffered qualms at this point for, although George stood rapt in contemplation of Amelia's face, strange though it may seem, it was not the ungainly blemishes thereon which thus riveted his attention, but her delightful upturned nose. Perhaps it was not surprising that he had omitted to remark it upon the night of her arrival at Carnleigh, for her face had been for the most part buried in her cousin's cloak.

The urgent repetition of Miss Winstone's enquiry brought him swiftly down to earth.

"Oh—er—yes, ma'am, the fever . . . quite so," he faltered, his eyes perusing the rest of the patient's countenance. "But what of the pocks?"

Diane heaved a sigh. "Yes, I agree they do look rather unsightly at present, but you must agree that were Amelia suffering from the small-pox, which you suspect, she would look a deal worse?"

George grudgingly conceded this point.

"Furthermore, Mr. Shadwick, I do assure you that these blisters will begin to disappear completely in a day or so—"

"Confound it, I can't wait that long!" remonstrated George, striving to subdue his voice. "It's too risky by far. Nicky will be a raving lunatic by then!"

"Isn't there anything we could do to convince him that the malady is not fatal?"

"With all respect, ma'am, that fact is not yet proven."

"I realise that, sir, but it serves no purpose to alarm your brother unduly. We must calm him somehow. Is there nothing you can suggest?"

"No . . . yes! Summon his physician! He'll convince Nicky if no one can."

"Alas, Mr. Shadwick, I'm afraid that would be impossible, and extremely imprudent," replied she, drawing George discreetly away from the bed to the door, lest their discourse disturb her cousin.

"But dammit, ma'am, my brother's life is at stake!" vituperated George. "You can't expect me to sit calmly by and watch him—"

"I sympathise most profoundly, sir, but to call the family physician, who could do little anyway apart from bleed him unmercifully, would be to court a terrible scandal. You forget the servants . . ."

"Servants?"

"How they gossip, Mr. Shadwick," she enlightened him in concern. "By summoning your medic you admit to the household what I have been at great pains to avoid, that the sickness is grave, and ere long your entire family would be ostracised by the surrounding populace with not a servant to do your bidding, all eager to believe the worst, as you yourself were."

"Humph," grunted George, realising the truth of this yet reluctant to admit so. "Then what do *you* suggest, Miss Winstone?"

"I do not presume to suggest what you do, Mr. Shadwick," Diane wheedled in typical female fashion, gradually manoeuvring him out of the door, "but beseech you in all earnest to put your trust in me. I swear it will not be misplaced. Believe me when I say in all sincerity, sir, that I know what malady ails your brother and will devote all my time and strength to making him well again which, God willing, will be in a few weeks. Moreover, if your brother does as he is bid, I guarantee to restore his complexion to its original flawless condition."

George stared at her in a mixture of perplexity, suspicion and surprise. True, he found it difficult to overlook the fact that she and her cousin were primarily responsible for the catastrophic situation, yet even he was forced to acknowledge a spark of admiration for her sound common sense and calm approach to the whole thing, especially after being carried off and threatened with imprisonment by two perfect strangers, not to mention how wearied she must have been after her fruitlesss journey, and anxious to reach her destination—and now, the added burden of her young cousin's health.

Though nought in the whole wide world would have made him confess it George found himself warming to Miss Diane Winstone and a pleasurable feeling began to surge through his being at the prospect of having her as a sister-in-law, and thoughts of brother Quentin's future being placed in such confident and determined hands. Indeed, a more determined wench he had never before encountered, George chuckled to himself whilst marvelling how he came to be out of the door and on his way back to his rooms without having realised it. Yes, a wench of obdurate spirit would be admirably suited to his elder brother, and would teach Quentin a lesson for treating himself and Nicky so shabbily.

But her popularity still hung upon the slender thread of Nicky's recovery. However, should she fulfil her devout promise and all be well anon, then George considered it politic to humour Miss Winstone and give all the succour he could to her whims and scruples, thereby winning himself a powerful advocate in his battle with the Earl.

Nevertheless, strange though it may seem, George's final thoughts as he lay composed to resume his repose

were not of Miss Winstone, Quentin, nor poor suffering
Nicholas, but of Miss Amelia Reynolds, and in particular, her bewitching, tantalising, delightfully tip-tilted
nose.

Seven

Fortunately for all concerned the heavily sedated Nicholas did not begin to rouse until the following evening when Miss Winstone was immediately on hand to deal firmly with any renewed outbursts of hysteria, which most certainly would have resulted if his expression of wide-eyed panic was aught to go by as full appreciation of his dire fate stirred afresh in his fevered brain.

As Miss Winstone explained the facts to him in a calm forthright manner, he lay staring up at her like a frightened child, clutching the bed-clothes firmly to his chin, prepared to accept—though only half believe—her assurances that his disorder was definitely not of a fatal nature and that, if he did exactly as she ordered, he would be wholly cured within a month, with not a single blemish to mar his prized complexion.

This Nicholas found somewhat difficult to accept upon snatching up his replacement looking-glass to confirm the large ugly inflamed blisters running rampant on his face. Under these circumstances there was only one thing to be done, and Miss Winstone did not hesitate to do it. The glass, along with all other reflective objects in the room, was confiscated, the mirrorstand on the dresser was covered up, and he was flatly forbidden to look at himself until his nurse granted her permission.

Furthermore, she applied her own peculiar grey concoction, made up by the village apothecary, to Nicky's
face no less than ten times a day, and to his profound
dismay, locked away his cherished potions and cosmetics, and pocketed the key.

However, not only was the malady infectious but
equally so was Miss Winstone's rational manner and
implicit faith in her old nanny's remedy which had
withstood the powerful test of time, so much so, that
George and Nicholas soon found themselves acceding
to her every command in the devout belief that ere
long her confident prediction would come to pass, for
surely even Fate would not have the effrontery to gainsay Miss Winstone?

Meanwhile, George wrestled continuously with an
overwhelming urge to see once again the object responsible for accelerating his heart-beat to a galloping
hoof-beat, to wit, Amelia's alluring nose, and to this
purpose he was to be found at every available moment
hovering eagerly outside the young lady's chamber,
striving to glimpse through the open door as Miss Winstone came and went that which he could not spy
through the keyhole. As can be imagined, it was not
long before such anxious vigil was remarked by Diane
who misconstrued his feverish interest to be on account
of her cousin's state of health, and in particular,
whether or not the rash was diminishing.

So George was granted permission to enter the room
and assist Miss Winstone, who was greatly suffering the
consequences of the past hectic week, by sitting with
Amelia whilst she took her meals, encouraging her to
eat which she felt little inclination to do. At other times
he would try to cheer her doleful spirits by reading to
her, and generally indulged her fancies to recompense

the unconscious pleasure she rendered him in simply allowing him to gaze continually at that object of her anatomy which he found so exhilarating.

Sure enough, next day George found Miss Winstone's prognostication beginning to come true and that Amelia's blisters amounted to three less than the day previous, which filled him with overwhelming elation. Appreciably, he was by no means the only person overjoyed by the news. Likewise was Nicholas who insisted upon witnessing this miracle for himself to meet with a firm rejection from his nurse who forbad him to quit his bed for an instant. Nicholas obeyed without protest, his flagging faith in Miss Winstone suddenly restored in the stimulating knowledge that he too would soon be able to boast his recovery.

At this turn of events a feeling of relief and contentment pervaded Diane that evening as she quitted Nicky's chamber after seeing him settled comfortably for the night, for it would not now be very long before she and Amelia would be able to resume their journey to Thatcham. This feeling continued with her until approximately twenty minutes to twelve when, lo and behold, shrieks and yells again rent the tranquil atmosphere asunder. As before everyone scurried to Nicky's room including George who, labouring 'neath the effects of his nightly tipple, staggered and stumbled up the stairs in his eagerness to keep abreast of the stampeding servants.

Diane also felt obliged to answer the summons despite her extreme tiredness and state of half-dress, and so, joined the throng *en route* to Nicky's chambers trusting that the ritual was not to become a regular occurrence.

"What the d-devil ailsh him thish time?" George exclaimed, meeting up with her where their two passages converged. "Dammit! Can't be the poxsh—er—if you'll parburp-pardon my blunt shpeaking, ma'am."

Diane smiled her acknowledgment, for she had grown accustomed to George's raw tone, expletives and all, and his proclivity to the wine-bottle. Indeed, she inwardly confessed to developing a warm affection for the two incongruous brothers with whom she found herself strangely involved; George, whose bark was proverbially much worse than his bite, if he ever bit at all; and Nicholas, whose preoccupation with his appearance was really quite superficial and who, way beneath the affectation, was not far removed from the angelic child he looked.

Two footmen and Blakeson were gazing about Nicky's bedchamber nonplussed when George and Diane came on the scene, whilst Nicholas screeched orders from the bed.

"Thieves! Brigands! Murderers!" he raved like one possessed, as George and Diane rushed into the room enquiring what was ado. "'S life, attacked in me bed! A great black shape, ten foot tall, damme, an' twice as wide, climbed in me window a-an' came for me! Would ha' been done t' certain death if I—"

"Sh-Sh, Nicky! Do calm yourself and tell us slowly what has happened," besought Diane, unable to comprehend a word of his gibberish.

"Aye!" seconded George peevishly, lacking Miss Winstone's tolerance and sobriety. "What the devil'sh the matter—"

"Brigands, I tell ye!" he shrieked, pointing with trembling forefinger into the far corner of the room which housed a ponderous oak-pannelled Jacobean cupboard. "See yonder cupboard, quick!"

George sobered considerably at this, though he remained sceptical.

"Don't be an idiot, Nicky, there's no one there!"

"Yes! Yes! Behind the cupboard!" persisted the distraught Nicholas.

"Nobody could possibly squeeze behind this cupboard," retorted George, subjecting the cupboard in question to a thorough inspection. "'B' gad, it's barely three inches from the wall."

"*Inside* the cupboard, then! Search it! He must be in there somewhere."

"He can't be, it's locked—halloo, what's this? No it isn't! It's being held shut on the inside by some . . . one . . . or thing!"

George was now cold sober and fell silent as the two footmen sprang to his aid. Together the three tugged at the door which flew open of a sudden to reveal a mysterious figure shrouded in black, clinging to the other side.

"Got you!" cried the three in unison, laying rough hands upon the criminal who emitted an inarticulate cry.

"'Pon oath, Nicky's right!" exclaimed George aghast, ignoring the writhing culprit's supplications to be released.

"Told ye so! Told ye so!" chanted Nicholas in gleeful satisfaction, bouncing up and down on the bed. "Unmask the rogue, George. Expose the dastardly villain! Let's ha' some jolly sport!" But the eager anticipation slowly congealed upon his countenance as the cloak was dragged from the struggling, biting, kicking intruder, exposing not the villain expected but: "P-Petronella? Wh-What in the name of—"

"Nicky! Nicky! Save me! Save me!" she cried in

tearful alarm, running to throw herself into his protective arms, to find her way barred by Miss Winstone who had rapidly recovered from her stupefaction.

"You must not touch Nicholas," she cautioned the girl, gently but firmly.

"Not touch him?" echoed Petronella, recoiling, her wide blue eyes shuttling betwixt Miss Winstone and the object of her desire as if trying to establish some relationship, whilst clutching a bundle of personal effects to her palpitating bosom. "B-But why not? He's mine! I love him and we are to be wed!"

"Aye, we're t' be wed!" confirmed Nicholas.

"Even so, Miss—er—"

"Great galloping gladiators!" ejaculated George, retrieving his senses. "It-It can't be!"

"I am Miss Petronella Wilchards, daughter of Sir Jason Wilchards," pronounced she, with a proud toss of her golden head.

"Good heavens! So you're Nicky's latest diversion," remarked George, staring her up and down.

"And you, sir, cannot possibly be Lord Carnleigh for he would not be so uncivil. Therefore, you must be Mr. George Shadwick."

"Honoured, Miss Wilchards," bowed George.

"Stap me vitals, Petronella!" broke in Nicholas, loth to be excluded and outshone by brother George when it was himself she had gone to such inconvenience to see. "What brings ye here? And in the dead o' night? 'Pon rep, girl! Ye might o' happened some mischief. No tellin' what skulks around these parts in the nocturnal hours. Egad, 'tis rumoured a headless spectre haunts yonder woods—"

"Oh, N-Nicky!" she cried in alarm. "How can you say such wicked things to frighten me after I have come all this way, shook to pieces on wagons and hay-carts, and nigh run off my legs—er—limbs, though 'tis not the thing for a lady of my station to admit—"

"But hang me," cut in George. "Why have you come here on this particular night? And at ten minutes to midnight?"

Petronella turned her disapproving frown upon her future brother-in-law.

"I'll thank you to keep a civil tongue when addressing a lady, George Shadwick," she rebuked him, tartly. "If you must know, though it's none of your business, I have run away because my father insists I marry Lord Pottle without delay, and has instructed my Aunt Emiline—"

"At Biggleswade," interjected Nicholas, helpfully.

"Biggleswade!" cried Diane, incredulously. "Y-You travelled all the way from Biggleswade unescorted?"

"Yes, ma'am," acknowledged Petronella, glancing down sadly at her bruised, aching feet.

"Instructed your Aunt Emiline?" prompted George, wanting to proceed with the narrative which boded interesting.

"You poor child!" exclaimed Diane, wringing her hands in concern. "You must be quite exhausted."

"I confess, I am a trifle wearied," sighed she. "But truly, it was beyond all to arrive here and be laid violent hands upon for a common felon—"

"Well, what do you expect if you go about creeping in windows like one!" parried George, bluntly.

"I did not creep in like a felon!" retaliated Petronella. "I *fell* in because my hood had fallen over my eyes and—"

"Yes, we know all that," goaded George. "You got as far as your Aunt Emiline, dammit."

"George!" censured Miss Winstone, strongly.

"Er—your pardon, I'm sure," he grudged gruffly.

"Yes, my father instructed my Aunt Emiline to lock me in my room until I should come to my senses."

"And did you?" breathed Nicholas, agog.

"Of course not, Nicholas! That's why I had to run away and come here . . . to . . . to . . ."

"Well? To what exactly?" urged George, utterly disregarding the fact that Miss Wilchards did not happen to be addressing him.

Petronella gazed apprehensively round at the anxious faces, which included Blakeson and the two footmen who were just as agog as everyone else though endeavouring not to show it, before she confessed timidly: "—to elope."

"Elope!" came the chorus, and Petronella flinched.

"My dear child, you can't possibly elope!" exclaimed Diane, placing a sisterly arm round the young girl's drooping shoulders. "Not tonight, any wise," appended she, discreetly.

"But we must! Y-You don't understand, ma'am, I've left a note! And when my father—"

"A what?" ejaculated George and Diane in unison.

"Oh p-please don't sh-shout at me . . ." she whimpered, turning appealingly to Diane. "Please, ma'am, won't you let me go to Nicholas?"

"I'm profoundly sorry, child, but I'm afraid it would be most unwise. Alas, Nicholas has contracted a sickness which is rather catching, and I'm certain that Nicholas himself, as deeply as he evidently loves you," went on Diane with the utmost diplomacy betwixt the two whose open adoration of each other was clear for all to see, "would be the last person to wish you the suffering and despair which has been his unhappy lot this past sennight."

George was struck with amazement bethinking Miss Winstone almost as adept as brother Quentin at extricating herself from embarrassing situations. Meanwhile, Petronella gazed longingly at Nicholas, who gazed longingly back at Petronella, both appreciating the sound wisdom of Miss Winstone's advice.

"B-But you will help us, Miss—er—"

"Winstone," supplied Diane amicably. "Diane Winstone. You may call me Diane, but I implore you at this stage, child, not to question my presence here."

"—er—Diane, please? I beseech you, for when my father sees my note and is informed of my escape he will set out after me with the servants, like hounds after a hare! Might even call out the sheriff and his constables! And when he f-finds m-me he'll—"

"Yes! Yes! I'll protect you, child. Come now! You must not distress yourself," declared Diane, taking the forlorn little figure beneath her wing whilst inwardly debating how on earth she was to gainsay an irate parent when it really was nothing whatsoever to do with her, and not even her house!

Moreover, any day now the owner was likely to arrive and find her in this exceedingly compromising situation for which she would need to word a most convincing explanation. Diane offered up a silent prayer that there would still be sufficient time for her and Amelia to get to Thatcham before any explanation proved necessary. True, she had promised in all sincerity to protect Petronella but was unable to determine precisely how she was to accomplish this without making her own position even more precarious, for she could scarce linger at Carnleigh Hall awaiting the ad-

vent of the belligerent Sir Jason and his army of constables. Perhaps, if the situation became really acute
she could take Petronella to Thatcham and there shelter her until the threat of battle was over and Sir Jason
in more receptive mood, and so conducive to reason.
Meanwhile, she might do worse than to disguise his
daughter as a member of the household staff, possibly
a chambermaid, to allay suspicion.

Being of a profoundly romantic nature Miss Winstone was inclined to let heart govern head and therefore extremely loth to see the lovers confounded and
torn apart to live lives of abject misery chained in wedlock to someone else, merely to gratify the whim of
convention and a stubborn parent. In her own
capricious belief, everyone should marry for love. Each
and every Cinderella should wed her Prince Charming
and live happily ever after.

This, did she but admit it, was the prime contribu-
tory factor to her own maidenly status, for alas, her
Prince Charming had not yet chanced along . . .

Eight

The following morning Diane found herself in need of a further supply of her nanny's special recipe to ensure her patients' recovery. After weighing the idea of despatching a servant upon the errand to Carnleigh Village she decided against it lest the servant be tempted to gossip. All had been well upon the first occasion for no one but herself had been aware of Amelia's malady. Now that Nicholas had contracted the malady too, and the entire household was whispering and tittle-tattling amongst themselves, there was no telling where the rumours would end, or how the simple peasant folk thereabouts might misconstrue it all.

Loth to risk attracting attention Diane disguised herself as the supposed servant by discarding her hooppetticoat and donning a plain gown of grey fustian, over which she tied an apron of white lawn and draped a white gauze kerchief about her shoulders. With a bergère chip hat set upon her becapped brown curls and tied 'neath her chin, she ventured forth.

Although her standard of classical education would have evoked the highest commendation from Mrs. Montagu and her following, alas, upon the subject of thoro'bred horseflesh her knowledge was found to be somewhat lacking. Indeed, she could have enumerated upon the fingers of one hand without any difficulty how often she had sat upon the back of the noble animal, and consequently regarded anything other than a donkey or pony simply as a horse, something to transport man with the minimum amount of inconvenience from place to place.

Upon arrival at the Earl's stables she stood back awhile until a small group of ostlers had dispersed and passed out of sight, then crept along to the nearest stall. Unfortunately, this chanced to house Lord Carnleigh's most recent acquisition: his much prized stallion of pure Arabian extraction which had been brought from Arabia at no little expense and inconvenience to its owner. But to Diane it was a horse the same as all the rest. And being equally conversant with the saddling of the beast as she was the beast itself, she simply threw a saddle-cloth over its back, strung a length of rope round its neck and, after four futile attempts, managed to mount it successfully.

Although she managed to quit the grounds of Carnleigh Hall without occasioning remark she found, to her uneasiness ere she had traversed a mile further, curious glances being cast her way by the local gentry and peasantry alike, whose equinal judgement evidently excelled her own and who therefore needed no official proclamation to draw their attention to the fact that the horse she bestraddled in such ungainly fashion was no mongrel breed. And upon arrival in the village itself she was even more perturbed to discover herself soon the centre of attraction, as if she were a performing bear come to divert the inhabitants.

Unable as yet to determine the reason for such feverish interest, Diane cast a surreptitious eye over her humble apparel to ascertain if aught were amiss. But no, all was well in that respect, and her dress quite similar to the ruddy cheeked kitchen-wench marching boldly by her side.

There seemed little else to do but assume an air of casual indifference, which she did, tethering the animal securely outside the apothecary's shop before entering therein to submit to the owner her nanny's treasured recipe. As the dispensing of this took some tolerable while she wandered about the little shop viewing the variety of jars and bottles lining the walls, and soon quite forgot her popularity outside—until the door burst open all at once and in rushed an apprentice, eyes goggling.

"Miss! Miss! Come quick!" he shouted excitedly, pointing the way with grubby forefinger. "Som'un's priggin' yer 'orse!"

Unfamiliar as she was with thieve's cant, it was obvious to her at a glance that something was amiss in connection with herself, and so she hurriedly paid her reckoning, snatched the mixture from the apothecary, and hastened out into the High Street in the wake of the boy where, sure enough, three exquisites were besporting themselves at her expense with the Earl's noble steed, the most elegantly attired of the three actually upon the horse's back whilst his no less fashionably dressed companions cried encouragement, thus attracting a larger group of onlookers whose interest was waxing again, deeming it the greatest diversion they had seen since the village strumpet had been drowned in the ducking-stool last Shrovetide.

But their interest waxed no stronger than Diane's fury when her eyes alighted upon the little scene, and storming across to the three offenders she seized hold of the horse's rope and tugged the animal to a standstill, exclaiming angrily:

"How dare you! Get down you impudent wretch! Get down this instant, d'you hear? Give me back my horse or I'll—"

"Gad! What do we have here, Weldon?" ejaculated one of the two on foot to his garish friend, both gaping in astonishment whilst the third gazed down upon Diane from his lofty position with an even loftier air, subjecting her to the most humiliating scrutiny it had ever been her misfortune to endure.

"*Your* horse?" he queried with a sneer.

In one agile movement he leapt to the ground and bore down upon her in a huge stride, seized her by an arm and dragged her bodily nearer to the horse, to which Diane took indignant exception.

"Unhand me, you misbegotten barbarian!" she expostulated, wild with rage as she struggled desperately—though ineffectually—to free herself. "I agree that it is not mine personally, but I am no less responsible for it."

"Where did you get this animal?" he demanded, striving to choke back a rage which seemed to equal, if not excel, her own.

"It's none of your business!" she flung back, outraged. "And I'll thank you to release me at once or I'll call the parish constable!"

"By Lucifer, I'll call the constable myself and have you clapped in irons if you don't answer me, wench!" he declared furiously, shaking her until her teeth chattered.

"L-Let me g-go y-you uncivil . . . ised . . . b-brute! I m-merely borrowed the horse t-to come on an errand," she protested as best she might, appreciating even so, that no matter how fervently she proclaimed her innocence her menial garb would give her the lie.

"You lie!" he challenged sure enough. "You appropriated it from the Carnleigh stables—"

"Ecod! Water it down, old fellow," advised one of his friends. "The jessy won't fathom ye."

"By St. Crispin, I'd soon make her understand, given a chance!" declared the other one, rubbing his lecherous hands together.

But Diane did not require, nor desire, his assistance. Indeed, the gentleman's meaning was plain enough for even the humble populace to comprehend, who stood around rapt in awe.

"H-How dare you accuse me of such a thing!" she cried with resentment. "How dare you suggest that I'd stoop to such knavery!"

And flinging self-control to the winds she dealt him a resounding smack across his supercilious face with her free hand.

At first she thought he would strike her back, but although he was justifiably enraged, he seemed to be even more astonished, for no common kitchen-maid would have dared do such a thing.

"Might I enquire precisely who and what you are, my unbroken filly?" he rasped, gripping her arm the tighter.

"Aye, whose wench are ye?" seconded his first companion, bedecked in puce superfine and silver lace, with matching hat at a Kevenhuller cock, propped up by eight inches of frizzed toupee.

"Yes, b' George!" piped up the one remaining, no less foppish in beflowered brocade trimmed with gold braid. "Must belong to somebody, plague take me, ne'er have I set me orbs 'pon such tempting perfectly rounded b—"

"If I belong to anyone, it is to the Earl of Carnleigh," she interrupted hastily, trusting the sound of this name would discourage them, as she finally dragged her arm free. "I am in his employ."

Far from discouraging them, the news seemed to stimulate even greater interest.

"Are ye, be gad!" exclaimed Weldon.

"Trust Quentin, lucky dog!" muttered the other, whilst their arrogant friend showed a keener interest in the horse's mouth and fetlocks which he was perusing at some length.

" 'Sbodikins! I'll wager I can name the service she renders, eh, Digsby?" remarked Weldon, bestowing a knowing wink on the frizzed spark who joined him in a guffaw of ribald laughter.

Meanwhile, their leader, who seemed almost as unamused as Diane herself, stalked slowly towards her, a look in his eye so threatening that she instinctively backed several paces.

"Despite my modest attire, sir," she endeavoured to point out, now wondering why she had thought it such a splendid idea to emulate a servant in the first place. "I am not the low-bred female you obviously seem to think."

"Aren't you?" he parried, a cynical curl to his lips as his eyes swept her significantly up and down. "You perchance seek some odd diversion by frequenting Carnleigh in your present array? Or to establish a new fashionable cult?"

"Stap me, if 'twouldn't create a veritable riot at Devonshire House," chortled Digsby.

"You play a dangerous game, mistress," went on his friend in a sinister tone, his eyes piercing her from beneath the wide brim of his gold point-edged three-cornered hat. "Mayhap you are unaware that such grave crime merits even graver punishment?"

"B-But I have committed no crime," spluttered she, still backing apprehensively away from him despite her grim determination to stand her ground in the rather dubious belief that if one was truly innocent one had nought to fear.

The gentleman apparently did not agree as he continued to come towards her, the pleated skirt of his superbly-styled coat of pea-green velvet billowing gently on the frolicsome breeze, which also stirred the white lace cravat beneath his smooth cleft chin.

"Alas, the evidence stands yonder and is quite irrefutable, eh, gentlemen?"

A chorus of support greeted this opinion from friends and villagers alike, the latter eager for some sport to brighten their otherwise dismal lives.

"I doubt vastly if our friend Carnleigh would be overjoyed to learn about your savage abuse of his prize cattle."

Panic gripped Diane. She had much already to answer for to the Earl and for him to learn of this ultimate transgression before she had escaped safely to Thatcham would be more than her life was worth. Thankfully, he was still abroad on the Tour—or was he?

"Th-The Earl is still a-abroad . . . is he n-not?" she stammered hopefully, which for some odd reason evoked gales of laughter.

"Loth as I am to disillusion you, fair maid, I hear tell he is returned."

"Aye! Stripped me of nigh a thousand two nights agone at Moll King's, curse 'im!" declared Digsby, appending quite solicitously: "I say, mistress, are ye feelin' vapourish? Don't look at all the thing, eh, Weldon?"

The agreement was unanimous for Diane had suddenly gone as white as the kerchief about her shoulders.

"Well, what are we to do with the wench?" urged Weldon. "Or are we to stand here bandying words all day?"

"Only one thing to be done as I see't," pointed out Digsby practically. "Hie her hence to the bailiff."

The further burst of approval which greeted this caused Diane to tremble in earnest. The group was not very large, it was true, but large enough to turn ugly should the gentleman in green be also in agreement.

"One moment gentlemen! But not so hasty," he mildly admonished them, one white lace-draped hand sweeping aloft to arrest their eager progress. "The catchpoll is an exceeding busy member of the community—"

"Hear him! Hear him!" came the overwhelming response.

"Let us not trouble him with such paltry creature as this,"—here, a disdainful wave in Diane's direction, "but as good law abiding citizens do him and friend Carnleigh a service by dispensing our own justice!" A wink was imperceptibly bestowed upon his two companions who immediately leapt to his call, scenting some capital ruse in the wind, and which the residents were not slow to follow.

Meanwhile, Diane stood riveted to the spot, her hands clasped over her heaving bosom like Joan of Arc at the stake, wondering how she managed to get herself in such awkward predicaments without even trying, and what her dire fate was to be. Suggestions were not slow to come from the crowd, but the gentleman in green appeared to be already decided upon his course of action as he turned to regard her steadily, enigmatically, as if savouring that which he had in mind . . .

"I propose the wench grant the three of us a boon."

His words were drowned by a chorus of approbation.

"By Jove! What a stupendous idea!" enthused Weldon, deciding without any difficulty what his boon was to be as he ogled Diane quite brazenly.

"Who goes first?" queried Digsby, discarding his puce coat with tender care, in preparation to do he alone knew what.

"I do," responded their leader in a tone which no one wished to gainsay, already stalking towards his quarry who resumed to retreat, further, further, until she felt her back contact the hard stone wall of the Turnpike Tavern.

Rallying her remnants of courage, Diane drew herself up erect.

"If you presume to lay one finger on my person," she warned, a deal less confidently than she felt as she groped frantically about in her petticoat pocket for her potion. "I shall dash the contents of this . . . this . . . bottle in your face!"

The bottle now materialised and she assumed a stance with it threateningly poised above her chip hat, defying her would-be attacker to venture one step nearer—at which he hesitated, eyeing the bottle in mild curiosity, wondering how she intended fulfilling her threat with the cork still firmly in position.

As the gentleman had no way of determining that the bottle contained an innocuous concoction of chalk, camomile, flower-water and powdered oyster-shell, and not some lethal acid such as Oil of Vitriol which was in common use, he was not prepared to take any risk. And so, as a breathless hush descended upon the audience, Diane suddenly found her arm pinioned in a brutal grip and her precious bottle wrested from her fingers. She uttered a cry of protest but too late, for he already had the bottle uncorked and was cautiously inhaling the contents.

"Oh *do* take care, sir, lest you drop it, I implore you!" she exclaimed in alarm whilst tenderly soothing her affected arm. "I have no money to purchase another supply, and it is of the utmost urgency."

"Why, what is it?" he questioned sceptically, glancing askance at the greyish mixture.

"It is a very special potion for someone who is extremely sick. Needed to save his life!" she appended on afterthought, hoping to shock him and everyone else out of their apathy.

"This? Save life?" he rallied her with a grimace of distaste. "Faith, if the aroma is aught to go by, I'd as lief suffer the sickness. And who may I ask is the hapless victim?"

"His lordship's youngest brother, the Honourable Nicholas Shadwick."

"Lies! She lies!" chanted the gathering, loth to let their chance of diversion slip away.

"She's lyin', like she did about the 'orse!" shouted a voice from the rear.

"Aye," another took up the theme, "It's poison to kill off the whole Shadwick family!"

"No! No! I swear, 'tis not!" Diane vindicated herself passionately, as Weldon sauntered up to place a confidential hand upon the gentleman's arm.

"Heed her not, m' good friend," he murmured in his

ear. "The jade merely seeks to deceive ye to save her skin."

"I speak true!" she cried, taking furious exception to the false accusations raining about her ears.

"She's a witch! Put her in the pillory!" cried one.

"The stocks!" sounded another, whilst the rest suggested everything from the whipping-post to burning at the stake.

"I vow on my very life that my lord's brother does have the sickness!" protested Diane, on the verse of apoplexy.

"What manner of sickness?" cut in the gentleman sharply, a warning glint in his eye, defying her to lie.

Diane procrastinated, glancing anxiously around at the sea of hostile faces which made her cruelly aware of the dire emergency upon which her life hung, suspended like a dewdrop on a cobweb, also aware that she had in her power the means to save it by uttering just one word. A word which never failed to strike terror into the hearts of every man, woman and child, indeed, as it had done to Nicholas at the onset of his illness.

And so she blurted out for all to hear: "The small-pox!"

A deathly hush met the pronouncement during which Diane could all but hear the mechanical clicking of each brain as her words began to register, some more quickly than others, until pandemonium finally broke loose and the populace scattered in all directions, shrieking wildly and devoutly crossing themselves as they went, mothers with bawling babes under their arms, cripples hobbling on crutches, one and all falling over each other as they fled for sanctuary, and in less than a single minute not a solitary living soul was to be seen in Carnleigh High Street with the exception of Diane who still stood gazing about her, marvelling at the rapid retreat. Even the three exquisites had seen fit to evacuate the scene who, typical of their ilk, had appeared so fearless when threatening someone weaker than themselves yet who had been first to take to their fashionable red heels upon the very scent of danger.

Indeed, as she stood thus alone in the deserted street she could have laughed outright but for the fact that she still trembled in the aftermath of what her fate might have been. However, upon contemplating her return journey she was not very pleased to find the horse vanished along with everyone else, presumably the three exquisites. And so with a sigh of resignation she set off on the five mile trek to Carnleigh Hall, rattling her brains as she went concerning the Earl's unparalleled stallion, and how on earth she was to explain its mysterious disappearance.

Nine

It does not exceed the bounds of credibility to appreciate that Diane was somewhat out of humour by the time she reached Carnleigh Hall, almost two and a half hours later, for it was not an easy road on foot. Furthermore, having quitted the house unprepared for a five mile march her feet now boasted the finest collection of blisters in the county, and burned hotter than the midsummer sun which beat down upon her the while.

But neither blistered feet nor sun blazed more torridly than her anger as with every step she took she mentally reenacted her harrowing indignity in the village at the hands of the man in green whose unwarranted interference was not only responsible for the disappearance of the Earl's horse and her present discomfort, but her cherished bottle of potion for Nicholas and Amelia, which had been her sole purpose in venturing out of doors in the first instance.

And so, whereas her first inpulse had been to slink furtively back to her room via the servants' stairs lest anyone witness her humiliation, upon eventually reaching the Hall her sense of outrage dictated otherwise. Howbeit, had she yet desired to enter the great house unobtrusively it should have proved no mean feat for even as she trudged the last hundred yards the ponderous doors opened and two maids and a footman rushed out to meet her, devoured with concern for her well-being and impressing upon her how Mr. George had been anxiously pacing the Blue Drawing-room for the past hours, refusing to eat a morsel, whilst Mr. Nicholas and young Miss Amelia threw fits upstairs in their beds, all wondering whatever had befallen her.

Diane felt sorely tempted to enlighten them there and then but decided to savour the revelation of her experience until she had attained the ear of George who was in the best position of all to do something about avenging her much-maligned pride. After all, Carnleigh being a small village gave her reason to believe that he should be able to identify the three rogues, or at least trace their whereabouts for there must surely have been someone at the scene of the crime who knew who they were, that was, if anyone would now see fit to entertain the Shadwicks following her public declaration that the house was striken with the small-pox.

As she wearily dragged across the hall to the Blue Drawing-room with the servants fussing and fluttering about her heels. Diane rallied her dregs of strength to disclose her staggering news, whilst Jenkins hastened on ahead to apprise Mr. George of her arrival.

George stood wringing his hands in torment by the huge blue damask-draped windows as she entered and stormed across—despite blistered feet—to halt indignantly immediately in front of him.

"A brute! A fiend! A lunatic, has just savagely molested me in the village and absconded with your brother's best horse!" she shouted angrily at the harrowing recollection, as if he were a league distant rather than two feet, battling to suppress her raging fury for it was hardly George's fault, and there was little purpose in unleashing her wrath upon *him*.

It was some considerable time ere George could voice his stupefaction.

"M-Miss W-Winstone!" he stuttered anon. "Wh-What in heaven's name—"

"You may well wonder!" she stated in the same tone, before going on to relate, in all its sordid detail, the day's disastrous occurrence, ending with the theft of the horse. "It is iniquitous that such blackguards should be allowed to roam the countryside terrorising innocent people!" she went on, her fury in no wise abating. "They ought to be suspended by their thumbs from the maypole and pelted with garbage! I have never been so humiliated in my life! Indeed, were it not for the fact that we must keep the whole thing behind a screen as far as your brother Quentin is concerned I should insist that you relate to him the whole disgraceful incident upon his return, and have him take the commensurate action with the local Justice of the Peace! And I shudder to think what his lordship will say when he discovers his best horse gone, though, to be honest, George, it didn't impress me to any high degree. I vow I've seen stronger legs on a week-old chicken. Why he should choose to throw away good money on an insignificant undisciplined creature like that when he might have had a sound pair of nags and a chariot at less than half the cost, is quite beyond my comprehension."

To Diane's vexation, now that she had time to notice, George did not appear to be hearkening to her story with any application of mind. On the contrary, she was getting the unmistakable impression that he was actually wanting to silence her but at the same time was unwilling—or unable—to say so outright or make his meaning clear for some odd reason. He was certainly distorting his features and gesticulating in the most peculiar manner.

"Is something troubling you, George?" she queried at length. "A speck of dirt in your eye, perhaps?"

"Er—" —cough—"no, Diane, ma'am," he stammered like a nervous bridegroom, striving to force three fingers of his right hand through the bottom buttonhole of his spangled waistcoat.

"You're quite sure?"

"Hum—q-quite."

On this doubtful reassurance Diane continued, to George's inexplicable mortification.

"Never, I do solemnly swear, George, have I ever encountered such arrogance, such insulting conduct towards a lesser mortal, even amongst the lower classes at the Haymaking Revels! But I suppose I should never have ventured abroad in the garb of a kitchen-maid. Upon my word, it has certainly opened my eyes to the iniquities of the upper class at play." She paused, panting for breath, her bosom heaving in unison. And gulping in a further supply of air, continued. "I'm sure you'll agree that we simply must make every effort to recover the horse, George?"

"Er—g-gentle . . . man in g-green, you s-say?" he probed with reluctance.

"The most insipid shade you ever did see."

"Oh lud!" groaned George like a soul in purgatory, which Diane misinterpreted as a sympathetic sigh.

"I mean, you'll be hard pressed trying to explain the animal's absence when you brother returns. And that's another thing,"—another groan erupted from her listener. "According to this band of rakes your brother is already in England! Moreover, has stripped half of London of their fortunes the night before last!" She was a trifle piqued that the news did not stun George as she envisaged it might, but she rallied on undaunted. "Well George? What are we going to do? I agree, I can easily acquire another supply of Nicky's potion but what about Quentin's beastly horse? If common opinion is to be relied upon we cannot expect to see another like it this side of the Continent, which leaves us little choice but to hunt down this—this—reprobate and get it back. And whilst on the subject it would be no bad thing for you to call out the villian and make him atone for his impudence by pinking him where it hurts most! George! For heaven's sake, what *is* the matter with you?" she exclaimed impatiently, flinging down her chip hat on a chair and shaking out her long curls. "To look at your face one would think Quentin was standing behind me! If you feel unable to confront this scoundrel then please say so. I shall think none the less of you, truly." She heaved a sigh of forlorn hope. "I'd solicit Nicky's help but by the time he's well enough to give the miscreant what he deserves, the horse could be already chopped up for Michaelmas pies."

"Mayhap I could be of service, ma'am?" sounded an incidental voice from behind at this point, at which George hastily clapped his hand to his eyes and Diane swung round on her heel, her look of surprise turning to open-mouthed horror at sight of the speaker who was none other than the principal character in her tale of woe—the gentleman in pea-green velvet.

How long she gaped stricken thus, her face defying every adjective in the English language, would be impossible to estimate, but George thought it a lifetime.

So much so, that he began to wonder if she would ever speak again, which was rather unusual for Miss Winstone whom he had never known to be lost for something to say throughout their close, though brief, acquaintance.

There he sat, not six feet away, in his sumptuous green velvet and all his impudent arrogance! The root cause of all the trouble, inhaling snuff with a nonchalant air as if the entire world were hinged upon his convenience.

"What is this man doing here?" she exploded finally. "He is the very vulgar ill-mannered boor I have been preaching about, who knoweth not how to conduct himself towards a lady!"

With languid ease the gentleman progressed to his feet, unperturbed by her derogatory allusion to his person, dwarfing her five foot four inches with his six foot two, thus placing her at further disadvantage while Miss Winstone stood bristling, fists clenched ominously.

"Faith, mistress," he drawled in a tone as impudent as his manner, sauntering round to reappraise her as if viewing a piece of merchandise. "I have greater right than anyone to be here, though 'tis doubtful if the same could be said of your good self."

Unaccountable qualms began to assail her. "Why, sir? W-Who are you?"

"Hold hard a minute!" burst in George here, in as much confusion as the two concerned. "Don't you recognise one another? Quen? Diane? Confound it all, I thought you were supposed to be affianced?"

Diane's heart plummeted to her blistered feet as she started flabbergasted at the stranger, pivoting her head slowly from side to side as if this would transform him into some other being and make all well again—whilst the Earl stared back at her, indeed, every whit as surprised but managing to conceal it a deal more effectively.

"N-No!" she gasped finally. "I-It can't be! Y-You aren't the—"

"Misbegotten barbarian, at your service, ma'am," he acknowledged with an elegant leg, to which Diane curtsied to the best of her weak ability.

Calamitous appreciation of exactly what this implied did not take long to surge into her brain. This was the man whom she had openly insulted in Carnleigh Village before his entire tenantry; whom she had threatened to have arrested; whose horse she had abused; and whose face she had slapped, the evidence of which she fancied could still be seen in a faint pink blemish upon his cheek, or was it merely imagination? He was the man whose house she had turned topsy-turvy; and who was now to discover that she had, during his absence, usurped the hallowed place of his future bride. What on earth was she to do? Should she openly confess all and be found out in a terrible lie? Have George and Nicky's implicit faith and high opinion of her shattered beyond repair? Granted, it had been partially—if not entirely—their fault that she had lied in the first place, but since the fateful night she had been given ample opportunity to deny it when the crisis had blown over and they had all grown to know and trust each other. But instead, she had chosen to continue the deception, to foster false hopes in their breasts for they never ceased enthusing excitedly about the not-far-distant day when they would all be united in one happy family. Knowing this, how could she bring herself to so disillusion them? Even now, she could observe George from the corner of her eye waiting expectantly, hopefully agog for her to resolve the paradoxical situation.

But what was the alternative? To own herself the bride of the man who had all but seduced her in Carnleigh before the whole neighbourhood, and had laid violent hands upon her? And to view it from his side was no consolation, for what peer of the realm would relish the idea of being implicated in her little conspiracy? Unless the peer in question had something to gain . . .

Diane regarded him furtively through her dark curling lashes. No, she decided, she was not dealing with George nor Nicholas now. This brother was quite a different proposition—certainly not the type to go meekly off to bed when bidden to do so, or eat up his gruel. Indeed, she would need to implement every wile and strategem in her repertoire to persuade *him* to her will, furthermore, there was his legitimate bride to be considered. However, what she would have to say to the unorthodox arrangement Diane did not waste time refining upon for the future Countess could scarcely discover the plan in the duration of a week or two, by which time she and Amelia would surely be in Thatcham.

Meanwhile, as George gaped on, the Earl smiled wryly, obviously divining her thoughts for, understandably, he was as wise as she, waiting with an air of idle amusement for her to react in the manner he was mentally predicting, viz: to faint outright at his feet; dissolve in tears; claim loss of memory; or plead an attack of megrims!

But my lord grossly underestimated the spirit and ingenuity of the female he was dealing with, for Diane resorted to none of these womanly deceptions, though to be frank, they did cross her mind. No, she recalled from her dear late papa that the essence of attack was surprise, and in this instance the adage appeared to prove worthy, for it took Lord Carnleigh quite off his guard.

"La, Quentin, my love," she exclaimed, tripping gaily forward. "I vow I did not recognise you in your new French wig?"

"Wig?" muttered George, as Diane threw her dimpled arms about the Earl's neck in the manner of an adoring bride but seizing the opportunity to breathe anxiously in his ear.

"Please do not fail me, my Lord, I beseech you in earnest! All will be lost! I shall be utterly undone!"

With her back to George only the Earl himself was able to witness the consternation in those lovely eyes, the desperate appeal of a maiden in genuine distress. Only he was able to appreciate the excruciating cost she was willing to pay in pride to thus humble herself before one who had that very day humiliated and degraded her outrageously. True, he was as yet in total ignorance of her reason for so doing, but whatever it was my lord was assured that it had to be a sound one. It would put him to no great inconvenience to grant her plea, and as she had somehow already managed to convince George and Nicholas that she was indeed their future sister-in-law then it would demand but a modicum of effort on his part to complete the subterfuge. It was going to take some tolerable while to delve to the bottom of all that had evidently befallen during his absence, but meanwhile, he was willing to assume his role which he would surely find interesting, if not rewarding, merely to discover just how far this Miss Diane Winstone was prepared to venture to give conviction to her part. He was sure to derive something from it all even if it were nought more than a degree of amusement at the lady's expense.

Lord Carnleigh returned a cryptic smile which Diane interpreted as favourable and her frantic heart-beat steadied somewhat—until she felt his arm tighten round her slender waist. My lord was quick to observe the warning challenge which sprang into those alert brown eyes at this familiar overture and his smile broadened. Yes, this was going to prove quite a novel diversion.

"You rally me, dear heart. I do not happen to be flaunting a wig," he murmured back anon, kissing her lightly on the cheek in salutation.

"Phew, can't say I'm not relieved!" exclaimed the forgotten George, for whatever the disagreement, it now appeared to be amicably resolved. "For one moment you looked as if you were utter strangers! Gad! It's devilish absurd, ma'am, but I thought you meant that Quen was this confounded blackguardly fellow you were holding forth about—ha, ha, ha!"

Diane blushed to the roots of her hair but managed to bear up well under my lord's mocking eye.

"Good heavens, George! What could put such a ridiculous notion into your head?" she returned with admirable conviction—even venturing a little laugh in unison. "I would scarce liken your brother to the wicked rogue I encountered in Carnleigh."

"Faith, if you will pursue the bizarre pastime of frequenting the neighbourhood emulating a kitchen-maid, my love, you must learn to suffer the consequences," remarked the Earl. "And pray what is the reason for your so evident relief, George?" he went on, his attention revolving to his brother who still stood by the window grinning broadly.

"Well, if you must needs wed, Quen, and we're all agreed you must, then Di—I mean, Miss Winstone here, should do as well as any other, eh?"

This, coming from George, was a compliment indeed.

"You approve my choice?" mused his brother. "You think Miss Winstone should make Carnleigh a fitting mistress?"

"Yes by jingo! You couldn't have chosen better, Quentin! Ask Nicky! Wouldn't allow you to marry anyone else—not even if you had a mind to!"

"I see," pondered my lord, beginning to perceive precisely how the land was lying and wondering what, if anything, he was going to do about it.

Ten

Why a gentleman of the Earl of Carnleigh's distinction and wealth should willingly accede to her plan did not occur to Diane at this present time, so overjoyed and grateful was she that he had acceded at all. And whilst she and his lordship played their respective roles, Nicholas and Amelia continued steadily along the road to recovery, each danced attendance upon by the doting objects of their hearts at every opportunity—Petronella upon Nicholas, and George upon his Amelia, prepared, for true love's cause to risk contracting the sickness—now that it was amply proven *not* to be the dreaded smallpox.

Indeed, it did not take the Earl very long to detect in which direction the weather-vane was pointing amongst the four, and whereas he was agreeably surprised to find George acting in such close conformation with his own dictates (Amelia obviously being a well-educated young lady of good family)—he wished that Nicholas might have fixed his sights somewhat higher than a mere chambermaid, betwitchingly attractive as she was.

Neither was my lord very long in enquiring whether or not Diane had dispatched word to Amelia's aunt at Thatcham regarding the untoward occurrence, in order to allay her fears—to which Diane was forced to reply in the negative, though hasting to excuse herself by stating that she had in fact, been about to do so several times but wondered if the truth would not perhaps alarm the matronly lady even more. Apart from which, it would not now be many days ere she and Amelia would finally be able to resume their journey and allay the aunt's fears in person.

Little by little my lord extracted from Diane everything that had occurred since her arrival at his home—that is, everything except the mystery surrounding the arrival itself, and how she came to be dissembling as his betrothed—which she was loth to divulge, to his inward annoyance, and repeatedly begged him not to press her on the painful subject. As Lord Carnleigh was equally unsuccessful with George and Nicholas concerning the crucial night—despite the exertion of his authority to the full—and young Amelia could recall nought about the night in question apart from the fact that she had felt dreadfully tired and ill, he decided to temporarily relegate the topic to the back of his mind—to everyone's relief.

Regarding his brothers' mischief in London upon the heels of his departure, he was already more than familiar, having been contacted the very day he set foot upon English soil by a certain Jewish gentleman from the City who, having recognised the distinctive design of the articles in his possession, was anxious to return them to their rightful owner—for the appropriate fee, of course, plus handsome expenses for his trouble, going on to give an excellent description of the two gentlemen who had pledged them. Having half-suspected that his reckless brothers might react in this fashion when cornered, the Earl was hardly surprised, and so, settling for somewhat less than was demanded of him, redeemed the items and said no more.

Each day, my lord emulated the gallant beau to perfection, conducting his 'affianced' round the extensive grounds of his country seat, revealing to her the wonders of his aviary, aquarium, summerhouses, rose arbour, and orange grove. And when the weather chanced to be inclement he would introduce her to the wonders of his home—priceless sculptured pieces and works of art from Venice and Florence, the finest Chinese and Dresden porcelain, extensive collections of gold and silver plate, and not least of all, the long gallery where over eight generations of Shadwicks gazed down in lazy contempt upon the passer-by, descending from Sir Barnabas Shadwick, who had perished upon the block, down to the present fifth Earl, whose likeness, Diane timidly observed, did scarce do him justice.

Howbeit, the Earl unconsciously revealed something else to Diane, of more personal concern—something which she would never have credited upon their first encounter that far from being the misbegotten barbarian she had disrespectfully designated him, he was the very quintessence of gentlemanly conduct. Indeed, his manner towards her was beyond reproach at all times—except, of course, if he sensed they were being observed when he would venture to take her hand or arm—nothing more—and even then, apologised most profoundly afterwards. But oft-times she would turn to find him regarding her in a strange disconcerting fashion which heightened her colour and threw her into some confusion—a look she found impossible to describe yet which would seem to give the lie to his otherwise innocent demeanour, as if he were playing a shrewd game, had set a trap and were waiting, expecting to catch her unawares.

But this aside, Diane found herself warming to her host, finding it easier and easier to emulate the character she played, and began to applaud herself at being a much more accomplished actress than she had at first given herself credit for—not thinking to question why, nor even entertain the possibility that she could be in danger of losing her heart, in all truth. She was ready to confess that she derived considerable enjoyment from the little masquerade and looked forward eagerly to her daily rendezvous with the Earl—wondering if his lordship enjoyed them too, or if, perhaps, he were an even better dissembler than she?

Her first awareness that all was not well with her emotions chanced during dinner one afternoon. She deemed it strange enough upon entering the Dining-room to find herself about to dine alone with his lord-ship—George being privileged to share a meal with Amelia in the seclusion of her boudoir—but stranger still when halfway through the third course he request-ed her to position herself a little nearer to him—ad-jacently, in fact, to facilitate the art of conversation, and thus avoid any risk of rupturing their vocal chords by otherwise having to call half a league down the ex-tensive table.

Diane gracefully acquiesced only to find her new position somewhat discomposing for she could sense her host's steady gaze fixed upon her the while, yet to her surprise, discovered—each time she dared to flash a glance at him—his attention to be centred elsewhere.

But what was strangest of all occurred at the close of the meal when a footman bore in the customary wine and she accordingly rose to withdraw, for what should Lord Carnleigh do but lay a restraining hand upon her arm, inviting her to remain—though the determination in his eye would seem to give her little choice in the matter—and partake of a glass of cordial. Granted, she deemed it highly irregular as she obediently sat down again, but there was no one to bear witness—not even the dutiful lackeys positioned behind his chair and by the doors, who had all been dismissed with a languid wave following the advent of the wine, leaving herself and his lordship quite alone.

This cloak of secrecy prompted Diane to anticipate some vital topic, intended solely for their ears, and she was not to be disappointed.

"It may interest you to know, Miss Winstone," he began affably, "that I have not been idle since my return from the Tour."

"I-I beg your pardon, my lord?" queried she, in some perplexity as to why he should think she would be interested one way or the other.

"Though you are like to demur in the strongest terms, I have, natheless, been diligently employed on your behalf," he ambiguously attempted to clarify his meaning, his long white fingers artistically paring a peach to his satisfaction.

As this made Diane little wiser, she remained silent, but with doubts circulating deep inside that what he was about to divulge was not going to be pleasant.

"When I arrive home to find my house inhabited by utter strangers—no matter how comely," he resumed, a challenging note infiltrating his amiable demeanour, "I feel sure you will agree, that 'tis not unduly unreasonable in me to desire to know a deal more about them, and consequently, ferret-out all I can. Your cousin and your goodself have proved no exception."

Yes, she agreed that this was to be expected but it did not prevent her from turning an odd variety of colours, undecided as she was whether to be angry or penitent, for she had no way as yet of determining how much of her humiliating past he had cognizance of, and so she decided upon a mild combination of the two emotions, and quietly smouldered, availing herself of three large sips of cordial.

"Faith, there is no need for embarrassment, Miss Winstone," he ventured in condescending fashion. "You may rest assured, I discovered nought concerning either of you which might cause you—"

"With all respect, my lord," intercepted she, piqued that he should witness her shame, "surely that would depend upon the agility of your ferret and the depths he was able to penetrate?"

Lord Carnleigh suppressed a smile . . . "If there is aught to be unearthed, I promise you, he will succeed. But if you will bear with me I fancy you may hear something to your decided advantage.

Diane bobbed up with a start.

"Y-You mean, my c-cousin Jeremiah has died? Without an heir?" she burst out on impulse.

The Earl swept one eyebrow aloft in mild surprise.

"I'm afraid not, but perhaps the next best thing—"

"H-He's on his death-bed? Writhing in torment with a ball lodged in some vital organ?" pursued she, agog. "Or has been bitten by a mad dog and carried off to Bedlam?"

His lordship gave a grimace of distaste.

"Loth as I am to disillusion you, ma'am, alas, the gentleman is apparently in excellent health."

He watched the rapture die from her face as her heart sank in despair.

"You are not enamoured of cousin Jeremiah, I take it?"

"No, sir," was all she responded, though her bosom swelled and her eyes flashed in accompaniment.

The Earl was not satisfied with this non-committal answer. He had expected much more, for the question had been designed to provoke her to speech. Unfortunately, this left him no alternative but to probe for his information like a hardened surgeon.

"I hear tell, that the ill-feeling you bear your cousin is not without foundation?"—he noted her fingers slowly curling into tightly clenched fists in her lap, which was the only reaction she gave. "For, an I much mistake, he inherited your father's title and estate . . ."—still she did not rise to the bait—"which, but for an anomaly in the law of the land, would have been yours, would it not, Miss Winstone?"

For one pregnant moment cool grey eyes held flashing fiery brown.

"Your ferret has worked well indeed, my lord," she rejoined with acrimony. "No doubt he has already been adequately rewarded."

Lord Carnleigh acknowledged the point with an inclination of his well-groomed head, as he brushed a speck from his cinnamon superfine with an indifferent hand.

"However, you might do well to consider that your cousin has committed no crime. 'Tis not he who stands at fault, you appreciate, but the law."

My lord was not to be disappointed, having taken pains to pink her in her most vulnerable spot.

"Then it ought to be revoked!" she exploded at last, unable to endure the possibility of Lord Carnleigh electing to stand in favour of cousin Jeremiah, and help wave his triumphant banner aloft in wholehearted support of the dominant male. "It is an iniquitous law which dictates that scoundrels like Jeremiah Figgis should snatch the better part of my father's wealth and possessions, whilst I—his own daughter—flounder upon a pittance!—forced to beg, borrow and steal my bread from others!—doomed to spinsterhood and some wry-faced dowager lady's companionship simply because I have no—" Diane pulled up short, biting her lower lip in vexation at having given way to weakness and allowed her emotions to overcome her sense of decorum.

"Well?" he prompted, searchingly. "Dowry?"

"I-I'm sorry, Lord Carnleigh—I-I crave your forgiveness . . . I did not m-mean to—"

"As you obviously hold the lot of a spinster in some degree of abhorrence," he smiled reassuringly, though more in amusement, "my news may come as quite a blessing, for you will be obliged to beg, borrow and steal no more."

"I-I don't understand," mouthed she, bewildered.

"Evidently your cousin is willing to atone for the injustice you suffer—though 'tis not his blame—by making you a most generous offer."

"H-He is?" she breathed with incredulity, for it was quite alien of cousin Jeremiah's nature to offer anyone anything.

"Indeed. Despite your lack of substance and past differences, he is willing to offer you . . . marriage."

Diane was struck speechless—speechless with rage that even Jeremiah Figgis should have the audacity—the effrontery—to make the proposal let alone expect her to accept it! Obviously, not content with seizing her father's other possessions he had a mind to seize herself too. How dare he! How dare he expect her to humble herself at his great clumsy feet, lay her all upon the church altar and assume the role of his dutiful spouse, bearing him child after child in order to ensure that *he* did not abandon the world heirless. No! No! Never!—not Jeremiah! She had deemed him intolerable enough as a child in the nursery they had oft-times shared, little realising how much farther he was destined to degenerate with maturity.

One glance at her face was sufficient to give Lord Carnleigh his answer.

" 'Twould seem your animosity is not entirely impersonal," he observed with candour, replenishing his glass with madeira. "You appreciate, nonetheless, that you are bidding adieu to your final opportunity to recover what is rightfully yours? To have your father's house and effects restored to you?"

"No, my lord," she returned with asperity. "They would never again belong to my family, not to the Winstones. From hence forth, they will always belong to—a Figgis."

No, she would never marry Jeremiah Figgis! Never! Not if he were the only man on earth!

But he was not the only man on earth. Indeed, in the past decade she had found herself infatuated with a veritable army of them—until they had overturned some form of physical contact (as impulsive virile youths needs must) when she had spurned them like rotten apples, unable to bear the thought of giving herself for life to a man she did not love. Even the innocuous act of taking her hand, or kissing her cheek evoked a feeling of revulsion in her, yet still she lived in daily hope that a certain gentleman would chance along who, when he took her hand in his, or kissed her, would not generate this feeling of nausea in her maidenly bosom—in other words, the gentleman she could love.

Nevertheless, she was ready to admit that her hope had worn a trifle thin during the last couple of years, until it now threatened to snap, hurling her into the abysmal depths of spinsterhood, for it was becoming increasingly apparent that no eligible bachelor, handsome, wealthy, or otherwise, would elect to wed a damsel so particular in her tastes, and whose ardour was scarce warm enough to melt a solitary snow-flake.

But it was at this point that a ray of sunshine pierced Diane's darkness of despair for the future, evoked by one thought—a sudden recollection of someone holding her hand in his, and kissing her on the cheek, without engendering the least resentment within her breast. On the contrary, she had quite enjoyed it, and secretly—though ashamedly—confessed deep down in her innermost being that she might have even permitted him to kiss her on the lips, had he ventured to do so, or anywhere else he fancied. And upon that rare occasion when his arm had progressed about her waist—purely in the cause of duty—her heart had given such a violent leap of elation that she was sure he must have noticed, thrilling her with the same profound feeling she now experienced as she awakened from her reverie to find the Earl standing before her with her right hand clasped in his, regarding her in that strange enigmatic manner peculiar to him. Furthermore, she was surprised to find herself standing too, for she could not remember rising from her chair, nor anything else save this inexplicable feeling which overwhelmed her at his nearness, his look—his touch!

Slowly, deliberately, the Earl raised the hand he held

to his lips, his eyes never deviating from hers, and Diane flushed, averting her gaze, striving to gainsay the uncomfortable sensation with the knowledge that it was all part of the play they were enacting—all a pretence—and that when it was over and done he would repel her just the same as any other member of his sex . . . at least she fervently hoped so. How could she ever survive the rest of her life if it were otherwise? And how diabolically cruel of Fate to awaken love in her heart for one who not only loved, but was about to wed, another.

Eleven

————◆◆————

Diane had not devoted much attention to the Earl's legitimate bride for whom he chose to marry was entirely his own affair and no concern of hers. And whereas she still persisted in this belief, she could not prevent the female in question obtruding upon her thoughts more and more as her growing interest in the mysterious damsel reared its disquieting head at all too frequent intervals, wondering who she was and why she had not ventured near her future home long ere now. Even had not good breeding forbidden her to ask outright, she simply had not the audacity to expect the Earl to satisfy her curiosity when she continually refused to satisfy his concerning the illicit occurrence from which the whole situation had evolved.

Howbeit, after taking her first tottering steps down life's emotional path Diane became a little reckless and proceeded to indulge in the precarious pursuit of reading hidden amorous interpretations into otherwise innocent gestures, looks, expressions, bestowed by the Earl, searching constantly for some sign—any sign—to appease the terrible gnawing in her heart, an ache she could not put a name to, nor quite decide for what. And although she strove valiantly not to lose sight of the fact that she was *not* the Earl's affianced it did not prevent her at the same time wishing more and more that she were, and after acting as such for the past two weeks was now dangerously near to believing it. Moreover, contrary to his touch repelling her modest instincts as her erstwhile suitors' had done, she was wishing he would actually overture the gesture more often. As he presumed to do this only when they were under observation and this, alas, occurred all too rarely during their walks which invariably took them out of view of the house, his lordship was not obliged to inject conviction into his role very frequently.

But something in his manner, she could not quite determine what, gave her leave to assume that he was not wholly indifferent to her, and were it not for the mortifying fact that he was pledged to another she was convinced he would sweep her into his arms and rain passionate kisses on her upturned face. Furthermore, if it should chance that she had somehow misconstrued his words and gestures out of all context, she still had one vital straw of hope to cling to, namely, the undeniable readiness with which he had leapt in response to her plea, volunteering to be a willing accomplice in the deception, which would seem to indicate that she exuded some fatal attraction, otherwise, why should he inconvenience himself so on her behalf, and at risk of losing his true bride?

Why, indeed! Diane was somewhat loth to delve too deeply into this lest she unearth something she did not like, something which might shatter her most ardent hopes, and like an ostrich preferred to bury her head in her dreams, telling herself that her prince would waken her with the proverbial kiss in the end.

For each assignation she took more infinite pains than the last with her toilette, and the following day proved no exception. She chose a billowing satin saque of the most delicate blue and draped it over large hoops—though not too large in case his lordship be discouraged from venturing close to her. Assisted by two maids she styled her hair quite elaborately like the ladies of St. James's, with a shower of ringlets caressing an exposed shoulder—provocatively patched —and whilst she readily owned that she lacked the peerless beauty of Petronella, she was nevertheless delighted to note that she had never been in better looks with not a single blemish to mar her complexion.

In eager haste she snatched up her fan and descended to the gardens despite the fact she was ten minutes early. As anticipated the Earl was not there, but she had not sauntered long amongst the roses, inhaling their delectable fragrance whilst struggling to subdue her galloping heart, when he appeared, seemingly as impetuous as she, and looking unnervingly handsome in a silver-laced coat of cerise brocade, exquisitely styled and complimented by ruffles of white Venetian lace at chin and wrists, whilst his rich dark hair lay lightly confined at the nape of his neck in a huge black bow.

Diane immediately averted her blazing cheeks, fighting to regain her self-control, and simulated an interest in a nearby shrub partly to convey the impression that he was taking her unawares but primarily to overcome her confusion, and embarrassment lest his fastidious taste and acute perception should detect that her gown, though flattering to her contours and of best quality, was not quite in the height of fashion and, having belonged formerly to Amelia who was of smaller stature, was threatening to split asunder at the seams.

Her heart reached bursting point as the tap-tapping

heels drew nearer, and suddenly there he was before her, bowing courteously over her hand and bidding his customary good-day, which she returned with a profound curtsy.

And so they strolled, exchanging pleasantries as they had done several times before, down through the rose garden and terraces to the avenue of tall willowy poplars where, to Diane's unalloyed joy, my lord's right arm gradually progressed round her shoulders, though his conversation remained commonplace.

She revolved head and eyes as best she might without occasioning remark, further thrilled to note that it was done for no other's benefit but, presumably, his own as there was not a solitary soul in sight and they were well out of view of the house. Indeed, she could well have swooned away at the feel of his hand on her flesh as his long slender fingers curled instinctively round her naked shoulder, such proximity bringing his face only a matter of inches away from hers.

Diane lost no time in putting her own interpretation upon this. Moreover, his mood was exceptionally genial, almost as if he had come to believe as much as she herself that they were actually betrothed and was no longer acting the part. Dare she hope? After all, he was keeping up the pretence purely to oblige her yet appeared to be quite enjoying it. What other satisfaction could he possibly derive from it all if he were not growing enamoured of her?

Emboldened by this sound reasoning Diane considered the moment opportune to encroach upon the hallowed ground of his true bride.

"You must surely be anticipating your reunion with your betrothed with some eagerness, my lord," she remarked, trying to affect indifference.

She felt his fingers tighten on her shoulder as if she had hit a vulnerable spot, but he chose not to comment and so she tried again.

"Does your future bride plan to visit Carnleigh Hall very soon, my lord?"

He turned to regard her through narrowed eyes.

"Why do you ask?" he parried suspiciously.

"B-Because if she is due to arrive in the v-very near f-future," she stammered nonplussed, "I must ensure that I am well *en route* to Thatcham ere she does so."

The Earl indulged in a cryptic smile, "Do I detect an element of cowardice?"

"That may be so, Lord Carnleigh, but I'm sure if I were she I should not take very kindly to another usurping my place."

"You would be jealous, perchance?"

Diane flushed a deeper hue than his lordship's coat and so she did not see much point in denying it.

"Y-Yes, my lord."

"Faith, I commend your honesty but why should she be jealous, think you?" queried he nonchalantly, plucking a red rose and inhaling its delicate fragrance, his right arm still draping her shoulders. "Do you consider I should have paid court to you more assiduously? Bestowed upon you more compliments? Wandered thus with you more often?" With his eye focused upon the rose he could not witness his companion's confusion and how she was gradually weakening as he enumerated each move in the repertoire of the practised seducer. "Mayhap, held your hand longer?. . .caressed your cheek more generously? . . . kissed you with greater fervour?"

Her brain suddenly reeled beneath this load of intoxicating possibilities and she threw open her fan to cool her fevered brow at a rate of ten flutters per second.

"M-May I prevail upon you to answer my question, Lord Carnleigh?"

"If I may prevail upon you to answer mine," he countered calmly.

Diane bit her lip in annoyance for giving licence to her natural curiosity and allowing him to snare her thus, for there was no mistaking his allusion to her mysterious advent at his home.

"Alas, my lord, i-if it were in my power to do so without wounding others . . . I-I should not hestitate . . . but I'm afraid—"

"As you will," he cut her short. "My contracted bride will not be arriving in the near future," he added in the same curt tone, removing his arm.

"How droll it should be if she and I chanced to be acquainted," she declared, endeavouring to inject the lighthearted vein back into the conversation. "We may have attended the same academy."

"That, I gravely doubt," he murmured deflatingly.

"Contrary to outward impressions, my lord, I ranked with the highest in the land at Dame Pocklington's!" exclaimed she, taking umbrage at his disparaging tone but perhaps more at the removal of his arm from about her shoulders. "Which you would already know had your ferret acquitted his task as diligently as you would have me believe! And permit me to add that Dame Pocklington herself deemed my execution of the famed Johann Sebastian Bach's two-part inventions and prowess with the pastels second to none! Furthermore, although I am obliged to give you the profoundest satisfaction and admit that I have descended a rung or two down the social ladder, as you well know this is due entirely to the iniquity of the law and the reprehensible crime I have committed in being born a female!"

"You misunderstand," was all he returned to the voluble outburst.

She fell silent, nuturing hopes as they strolled by the Great Lake that he might clarify the misunderstanding, but in vain.

"I-I'm sorry, Lord Carnleigh," faltered she anon, feeling rather ashamed of herself, "I really ought not to have spoken out as I did just now, but I find myself very confused, wondering why you choose to serve me thus? Allowing me to pose as your intended bride?"

"It pains me to disillusion you, ma'am, but 'tis not done entirely for your benefit," he replied bluntly. "In obliging you, I also oblige myself."

"I-I don't follow you, my lord. What pleasure can you derive from enduring my irksome company day after day? Not to mention the dire risk you court of having your true bride discover all."

The Earl turned abruptly away as if his conscience troubled his peace of mind, and again Diane suffered qualms that she had blundered and incurred his displeasure.

"Lord Carnleigh! I swear I did not mean to encroach upon such private and personal matters," she avowed in earnest, writhing inwardly at having exceeded the bounds of propriety and ruined her golden opportunity. "In all honesty, I plead acute concern for your own future happiness my excuse, lest in so gallantly assisting me you peradventure offend—

Her voice trailed pathetically away to end on a ner- or even lose—the one . . . y-you . . . l-love most . . ."

vous tremor for his eyes were upon her, seeming to read more into her confession than she intended.

But then my lord smiled, and all was well, as he casually cast aside his depression along with the rose.

"I thank you for your so generous consideration," he responded affably with a flourishing bow, "but I assure you, there is not the slightest cause for concern on my account. And whereas I am deeply touched by your sense of loyalty to me, I am loth to tell you, Miss Winstone, that 'tis quite misplaced."

"But your affianced . . ."

Lord Carnleigh gave way to a chuckle. "My affianced? Ha! There you have e'en less reason to be concerned," he mused philosophically. "Faith, how can one lose what one doesn't possess?"

With that he ambled on down the neat flower-bordered path leaving her to follow on.

But Diane was unable to follow even had she wished. She stood rooted to the spot like an adjacent stone statue, wondering if she had heard aright, pinching herself to ensure that it was not all a dream as her head spun round and round—until it suddenly cleared and the full import of his words and all they implied flooded in to take possession of her.

He was free! Free! He was eligible! She could cherish hope, at least more hope than she had cherished hitherto. She could—and indeed would—have cried it aloud to the very heavens in sheer unmitigated joy but the Earl had turned and was wending his way back, which prompted her to act with the utmost caution, lest she inadvertently betray her true feelings.

Uplifting her voluminous petticoats she hastened to meet him, pleading that she had lingered to admire the marble and gold sundial, and managed to seem outwardly calm, with the exception of her fluctuating bosom.

"F-Forgive me, my lord, b-but do I comprehend correctly?" she asked breathlessly. "Do you say that you are not, after all, betrothed to wed?"

"Your understanding is excellent," he accorded pleasantly.

"But your brothers—you would have them believe that you are?"

"'S life, I must also compliment your perspicacity," he rallied her. "Aye, there you have it."

Granted, the news was wonderful in one respect but in another quite disastrous! Until this crucial moment Diane's solitary wisp of hope had hung upon the comforting knowledge that he had undertaken the exacting task of emulating the love-lorn swain purely to accommodate herself, and for his own pleasure, the enjoyment of her company. Now, in one fell blow her dream was shattered! He had a powerful motive for acting thus because he was not doing it for pleasure but to steal a march on his brothers.

She was a fool! A foolish simpering schoolroom chit enamoured of her tutor! How could she have been so besotted as to imagine that a man so wealthy, so handsome and personable, head of one of the oldest families in England and able to command the entire society mart, would design to fling his handkerchief in her direction?

Slowly, she could feel her life's blood, or something very akin to it, draining away, carrying her last shred of hope with it, leaving her miserable and forlorn.

"Why?" The monosyllable almost choked her.

The Earl meandered to a halt in the middle of the stone ornamental bridge spanning the lake, and leaned indolently on the parapet, gazing down upon the virgin-white swans sailing serenely on the calm waters.

"It has long been my ambition—since I came into mine inheritance, in fact—to be permitted to live my life according to the dictates of mine inclination, to indulge my whims and fancies at random with thought to no one as do the rest of mine acquaintance. A selfish ambition, you might think, but no more selfish than that of my younger brothers whose reckless living would have ruined me in the not-too-distant future."

Diane stood dejectedly by his side, unable to tear her eyes away from his pale handsome profile as he elevated his gaze from the floating clouds of white plumage below, to let it drift pensively over the panoramic landscape created by the famed William Kent.

"And so I fostered the falsehood, encouraged them in the belief that I was about to wed, to shock them out of their apathy, to compel them to abandon their wasteful pursuits, or find wives of their own—if not with wealth commensurate to their tastes, then with the ability to transform them into the doting dutiful spouses they ought to be."

A pang racked Diane. He was using her to cling to his bachelordom! She now almost wished that he had indeed been betrothed for at least her enemy would have been something tangible, visible, a fellow female whose power of attraction she could have assessed. But to be expected to pit her ingenuity and strength against this unseen force was to admit defeat from the outset.

She stood before him, her heart burdened with remorse, but the only indication of this was to be found in her eyes, which she kept discreetly lowered as he turned to her.

"You do not envisage yourself in the role of doting

dutiful spouse, my lord?" she probed in a distant voice, not at all like her own.

"No, until I needs must," he answered decisively. "Of course, no doubt you appreciate, if George and Nicholas were to discover this they would feel at liberty to follow suit?"

Here, Lord Carnleigh wrenched the knife in her wounded heart by taking her hand gently in his, oblivious to the agony he was causing her.

"Needless to say, Miss Winstone, I should be deeply in your debt if you would condescend to respect my confidence and continue to act this 'Comedy of Errors' a while longer," he besought her, his voice barely above a whisper, and standing so close that she could feel his warm soft breath on her burning cheek. "It cannot be very long now. I sense marriages on the grapevine. You must have remarked George's *tendre* for your cousin, for example? I must own, I did not anticipate upon my return finding him in particular so stricken by Cupid's arrow. However, I must point out lest you wrongly assume his feeling to be engendered by your cousin's fortune, that apart from George being quite in ignorance of Amelia's wealth, he himself is not as impecunious as he believes, nor Nicholas. Unbeknownst to them I speculated a portion of their substance upon an East India shipping venture, and am pleased to relate that I have reaped tolerable dividends, endowing them with a comfortable—if not lavish—annual income of approximately five thousand pounds apiece.

"H-How nice," she faltered weakly, for though the news was all very delightful to those concerned it did little to lighten her own burden. "I trust Amelia's papa will be persuaded to come about as, despite her plain looks, I suspect he covets a title for her."

"Alack," opined the Earl. "I'll warrant he won't be over zealous, then, when he meets George."

"I promise you, my lord, I shall try my utmost to wring approval from my uncle who, I add in all humility, respects my opinion. And I feel I know your brother sufficiently well to be able to vouch for him whole-heartedly. Indeed, I vow his character is quite reformed for I have seen no evidence whatsoever of reckless behaviour—er—more recently," she appended hastily, to avoid a blatant untruth, for there had been ample evidence upon the night she arrived, "—and I personally consider the two excellently well suited."

The Earl smiled his acknowledgement, tightening his grip on her hand as she tried to remove it from his possession.

"I should be further indebted to you if you could accomplish such a miracle. Faith, if only some good fairy would cast her wand in Nicky's direction. 'Twould appear in his case that he is about to leap into the fire from the proverbial frying-pan."

"How mean you, my lord?" she enquired with a glance of surprise.

His lordship heaved a sigh. "Surely you cannot have failed to observe how he continuously solicits the company of a certain fair menial in my employ? An undeniable jewel, I grant you, but scarce worthy to bear the Shadwick name."

"But Nicholas is pledged to Petronella and is truly devoted to her, Lord Carnleigh," Diane sought to acquit the two honourably without cruelly betraying their secret.

"Indeed? Then it harrows me to think what Mistress

Petronella's opinion would be of her so ardent admirer were she to spy him dallying with the chambermaid. Petronella? Hm-m . . . the name carries a familiar ring . . ."

"Wilchards, my lord."

"Ah! Daughter of Sir Jason, an I doubt not."

"You have met Sir Jason?"

"I'm afraid not," responded my lord, unmistakable relief in his voice as he cast her a sheepish glance. " 'Tis a pleasure I have thus far managed to elude."

Diane could not resist a smile despite her heaviness of heart.

"You find yourself—er—privileged to boast the acquaintance of this paragon?" resumed the Earl with interest as they turned to make their way back to the house.

"I consider myself extremely privileged, my lord, for not only is Petronella an accredited beauty by society's exacting standards, but heiress to a not inconsiderable fortune," declared she, hoping she had not divulged too much in her eagerness to impress. "Consequently, she may command the entire marriage mart and select any beau she pleases. Perhaps, even your good self, Lord Carnleigh?"

My lord elevated a disdainful eyebrow.

"My taste in females extends far beyond the superficiality of life, and I have no need of wealth," he returned with candour. "I require something more than mere beauty."

"What more could a man ask of a wife?" she countered swiftly.

The Earl swept his eyes aloft to the azure skies, pondering the question.

"Spirit," he announced decidedly. "An indomitable

spirit that I might call to heel when occasion demands. A female who does not dissolve in tears at the first sign of adversity, nor throw a tantrum when the wind happens to blow the wrong way."

Silence dogged this interesting revelation as they approached the parterres, Diane noting curiously that his list of requirements conformed very closely with what she had always regarded as imperfections in herself.

"However," he went on in more rigorous tone, as if suddenly recalling his duty, "she must, before aught else, accept her position as my wife and conduct herself as befitting a peeress, which means withstanding all manner of provocation. A great deal to ask of a spirited female, would you not agree, Miss Winstone?" he probed, eyeing her calculatingly.

"Not if she were also gifted with common sense, my lord," she parried, calmly meeting his challenging eye which, strangely, seemed to cause him some mild embarrassment, and he turned away to feign an interest in the flower baskets suspended from a stone archway.

As they finally neared the house Diane found the strain of her emotional turmoil beginning to take its toll, the constant battle to withhold her true feelings lest she utterly betray herself was too much, and so she now longed to retreat to the haven of her room—but instead, the Earl chose to detain her on the terrace.

"I would endeavour to thank you for all you have tolerated during the past weeks," he stated gently. "It cannot have been easy."

Gratitude! His gratitude! She could suffer anything but that—even his wrath!

"As I said earlier," he continued in the same intimate tone, undermining her remnants of resistance to an alarming degree, "it cannot endure much longer.

Your cousin is to quit her room tomorrow so I see no reason why you both should not be gone next week."

Oh no! She could not bear the thought of leaving, not so soon! It was intolerable! Although it pained her to be with him, it was not to be compared with the agony she knew she would suffer without him, knowing she might never see him again, certainly never to recapture the little intimacies they had shared—his expressions, gestures, meant only for her.

"I-I'll be—er—I mean, w-we'll be s-sorry to—to—leave," she managed to stammer, so confused that she could not decide whether she wanted most in the world to throw herself bodily into his arms and give licence to her heart, or take to her heels and run away out of his life forever to a place of seclusion where she would never hear the name Carnleigh again. "A-Amelia especially, sh-she'll be extremely loth to leave G-George . . ."

"Thatcham isn't far," he observed lightly. "There is no reason why George should not visit her frequently, with her aunt's permission, of course."

He hesitated, regarding her steadily, prompting her gaze to flutter round the gardens from flower to flower like a butterfly unable to make up its mind precisely where to alight.

"But what of yourself?" he pursued with discretion. "Do not you also wish to tread the nuptial path in keeping with the rest?"

The blood rushed to her cheeks, for his tone was faintly mocking, though his expression remained quite serious.

"I am not at liberty to indulge my wishes, my lord," she replied in a humility which pained her sorely. "I do not boast a handsome portion like others."

"I stress, you have earned my gratitude for which I am willing to recompense you in whatever manner you think fitting. Even to the extent of furnishing you with the necessary dowry—or husband, for that matter. Wealth and position unlock many forbidden doors."

Diane cringed inwardly. The very idea of what he was proposing was sufficient to send her galloping full tilt to the nearest nunnery, but how could she even begin to tell him so without wounding his pride.

"Thank you, my lord," she murmured simply. "I shall devote careful thought to your generous offer." The words almost choked her.

"Moreover, I believe that Nicholas also has excellent reason to be indebted to you for not only saving his life but something decidedly more precious to him—his complexion."

She smiled wistfully, bethinking this typical of Nicky, and for one brief moment her personal problem drifted to the back of her mind as she pondered the Earl's brothers whom she had already come to regard her own.

"Of course, Nicholas intends to thank you himself ere long—"

"Really, Lord Carnleigh," interrupted Diane, rousing from her day-dream, "I swear, there is nothing in the world for you or Nicholas to thank me for. I did no more than anyone would have done in similar circumstances."

Lord Carnleigh returned a sceptical look.

"It is the precise nature of these circumstances which troubles me," he informed her dryly. "It would appear there lies a deal more behind his gratitude than anyone is prepared to admit. Even George seems anxious to thank you for something yet persistently refuses to say what."

Diane looked the personification of guilt as she fidgeted nervously with her fan of painted silk, aware that they had revolved full circle and were back once again to the crux of the matter.

"Am I to infer by your silence that you still refuse to reveal your secret?" he queried on a curt note.

"I do not presume to refuse you, Lord Carnleigh," she hurriedly replied in obvious discomfort, wishing with all her heart that the cracks between the paving stones would open and swallow her up. "However, I should prefer you not to press me—"

"Very well," he interrupted. "But you may rest assured, ma'am, that I do not intend to relinquish my quest. I small extract the necessary information from someone ere long, even if I must needs drag them belowstairs and turn them on the rack!"

And barely brushing her hand with his lips he swung round on his heel and strode indoors.

Twelve

———◆———

To Diane's overwhelming relief Lord Carnleigh did not seek her company upon the following day, nor the day after, granting her the necessary time for meditation, for searching into her heart, hoping therein to find some magical solution to her emotional enigma, something to rid her of this terrible burden, for although his lordship was the major cause, it did not seem that he nurtured intentions of administering the cure.

But not all her time was expended repining alone. Amelia had now abandoned her sick-bed, and whereas not yet fully recovered she was nonetheless quite able to partner her cousin in card games and conversation, the prime topic of which was, not surprisingly, betrothals and weddings, much to Diane's mortification. Even so, it was highly preferable to having Amelia probe too deeply into her own strange relationship with their host, which appeared to be the painful alternative despite the fact that she had long since sworn Amelia to silence on the vital subject. Of course, for the better part of the day Amelia was danced attendance upon by her doting George and it was only when he was physically dragged from her side on some emergency that she prevailed upon Diane to take his place, yet whose dismal company Amelia considered she might have fared better without.

To everyone's astonishment, the recovery of Nicholas was effected somewhat quicker, and no sooner was he out of bed than he was strolling (though multi-scarved and great-coated despite the fine August weather, lest he suffer a relapse) in the rose garden with his 'chambermaid'.

As can well be appreciated, Lord Carnleigh's deliberate shunning of his future bride did not go unremarked by all concerned, which in no wise served to ease Diane's unhappy lot, since she now felt herself the prime subject of every tittle-tattling menial from scullery-maid to head footman.

It was not until almost a week later, in fact, two days before she and Amelia were due to undertake their journey to Thatcham that the Earl condescended to extend the olive branch and request her—via his man—to meet him by the sundial at noon that day. Her initial reaction was to feign some plausible excuse, a headache or suchlike, in order to avoid what could be only an excruciating ordeal, a stringent test of her acting ability, and resistance to his deadly charm.

But this was the very type of female she had openly declared war against in the Earl's hearing, and upon reflection, found her inveterate sense of good breeding asserting itself, forbidding her to quit his house without expressing her thanks for his kind hospitality, for as host he was indeed second to none. Granted his motives would not withstand close inspection, but when one weighed the extreme provocation he had tolerated upon his return from the Tour, apart from Amelia giving Nicholas the pox, it was a miracle, in retrospect, how he had not ejected them instanter. After all, none

of the past weeks' catastrophic events would have come
to pass had not she accosted Nicholas in the first place
in the yard of The King Charles Inn—which, did she
but confess it, had not happened as accidentally as she
would have them believe, once she had discerned the
Carnleigh coat-of-arms upon the coach panel.

And so, Diane fulfilled my lord's explicit request and
ventured out promptly at the prearranged time to meet
him, her shapeliness clad in another of cousin Amelia's
cast-off gowns, though no less exquisite, of stiffened
primrose damask, worn over a fan hoop, the elbow-
length sleeves trimmed with double lace flounces and
the whole complemented by matching damask slippers
supported by two-inch heels. A beflowered chip hat enhanced her beribboned curls while her perspiring hands
nervously clasped a fan of painted chicken-skin.

As she quitted the house she spotted his tall manly
figure pacing the length of the lilypond just by the sundial, as if he were growing impatient, yet the hour was
barely noon. Diane did not venture to look at him
again as she crossed the terrace, descended the steps
and passed through the rose garden, and upon approaching him, sank into a decorous curtsy with a
whisper of silks, her eyes demurely lowered, due more
to cowardice than modesty. This, Lord Carnleigh
honoured with a stiff bow, merely civil nothing more,
and briefly suggested they repair to the orange grove as
Nicholas and his chambermaid were promenading close
by, and George was about to emerge with Amelia at
any moment.

Having said this he fell silent, not sparing her a second glance. Indeed, it was the longest he spake
throughout the entire walk, and moreover, when Diane
summoned sufficient courage to proffer her carefully

composed and well-rehearsed speech of thanks he did not condescend to repay her with as much as the courtesy of a smile, nor give the slightest indication that he had even heard it. As his eyes remained firmly fixed on some distant object she seized the opportunity to flash a glance at him, to instantly regret it, for her pulse accelerated to twice the rate and she again experienced that now familiar overawed feeling, the dissolution of her bones.

Never had she seen him look so handsome, his towering stately figure clad in a suit of lilac brocade, lined with sarsanet and lavishly trimmed with silver lace, the elaborate cuffs turned back to the elbow—whilst his unpowdered hair was dressed in the customary queue, and the finest Italian lace frothed at wrists and chin, emphasizing the strength of character in his clean-cut aristocratic features. Matching amethyst rings flashed upon the middle finger of each hand as he brushed imaginary folds from his whaleboned skirts, with impatient gestures.

Following the humiliating rebuff her speech had been accorded Diane was loth to grant him another chance and was therefore determined to make no further attempt to draw him into conversation and—as the feeling seemed to be mutual—well over an hour elapsed with not a word passing between them.

But the time did not elapse without adverse effect upon Diane's nerves, and neither, apparently, was she alone in the experience for the Earl commented of a sudden:

"You leave in two days?"

"Y-Yes, my lord," she stammered, undecided if it were a question or simply an observation.

"Your cousin is well enough to travel?" he pursued, his eye roaming in every direction but hers.

"So she assures me, Lord Carnleigh."

A slight pause ensued ere he appended laconically, "You will be missed."

"Thank you," responded she, more for something to say.

"I was not merely being polite," he saw fit to apprise her, with some difficulty. "My brothers . . . esteem you very . . . highly."

"And you?" she conquered an overwhelming urge to ask.

It was not until this moment that Diane realised how much the Earl had changed during their short separation, perhaps she had too, and could sense the inward battle he was fighting to regain that casual intimacy they had been privileged to enjoy hitherto, wondering—as did she herself—what had become of it? How it had escaped them? And why they were unable to recapture it?

As this seemed to be the end of the futile attempt to converse Diane retired inside her broody meditations, further dismayed by the thought that he had not once, during their perambulations, made any effort even to take her hand, and began questioning his motive for inviting her to take the air with him at all when he was obviously relishing it as much as she.

After traversing the orange grove they had since wandered along by the lake to the extensive orchards and were now upon their return walk through the neatly laid parterres. This necessitated passing by the huge ornamental foundation with its twin flights of stairs on either side, and as they approached, Diane's heavy-laden heart suddenly leapt with joy as Lord

Carnleigh took her arm, but alas, it was solely to assist her up the first flight of steps after which he immediately released her again. Bitter disillusionment at once engulfed her, dogged by deepest remorse, then anger, and as they crossed the stone dais of the fountain she spied the second flight of steps descending on the farther side, and instantly determined that, should he deign to offer his assistance again she would frigidly decline it.

The fact that this flight, unlike the first, was in some need of repair in no wise deterred Diane whose despondency and pride forbad her to recant her avowal.

As anticipated, upon arrival at the steps in question Lord Carnleigh offered to take her arm which she snatched away, stepping aside in resentment, and summoning every shred of dignity she possessed she descended one step, two steps, alas, stumbled upon the third and would surely have fallen to sustain injury—if only to her pride—had not the Earl been on the alert and caught her in his arms.

Their eyes met briefly, a look no words could describe, and before her feminine intuition could prompt her what to do next his lips were devouring hers in a kiss of wildest passion! Overwhelming her! Intoxicating her beyond belief! Drawing everything from her to feed the flames of his blazing desire, her very life, her soul, which Diane was only too willing to give as she clung to him in equal desperation, bewidered that this could truly be happening to her, the wonderful experience she had so often dreamed about—but never, never anything quite like this . . .

But just as suddenly it was all over, and the Earl recoiled several paces to stand staring at her in stupefied disbelief, stunned, one elegant hand, shaking visibly, sweeping across his forehead in an effort to clear his fuddled brain while Diane stared back, her eyes glistening with adoration. Indeed, her whole being radiated from her eyes, revealing openly for all to see the profound depths of her love, which a man as astute as his lordship could hardly fail to observe. She remained trembling before him, gazing up rapt into his confused eyes, waiting, tensed, breathless, hanging upon his lips for the ardent declaration of love which she felt was certain to follow such a violent display of emotion.

But no such declaration came. Instead, he dragged his eyes away from her to gaze all around him like one rousing from a metamorphosis, seeing everything anew, the birds; the trees; the shimmering water playing in the fountain; the whole landscape; as if half expecting them to have undergone a transformation too. However as his eyes swept aloft over the heavens, the look of wonder on his features gradually changed to suspicion . . . apprehension . . . then resentment, like a bear suddenly aware of the gin-trap on its paw. And when he finally spoke it was upon an underlying note of contempt.

"By the faith," he laughed tremulously, shaking the feeling aside, "I must congratulate you upon such a performance, Miss Winstone! It must surely have convinced our audience beyond any shadow of doubt."

With a cry of anguish Diane spun round, horrified to see the eager faces of George, Amelia, Nicholas and Petronella grinning in evident delight at the amorous display, over a hedge not ten yards distant. To suffer this monstrous humiliation on top of that accorded by his lordship was more than she could bear, and with a pitiful sob she snatched up her petticoats and fled the scene, battling manfully to hold back her grief until she reached the sanctuary of her boudoir where she flung herself down upon the great four-poster bed and cried as if her heart would break.

Thirteen

"Oh lud! Not another lovers' jangle," groaned George, voicing the opinion for everyone present whose expressions had fallen unanimously downcast, for the abject despair written upon Diane's countenance as she had hastened by could scarcely be misconstrued—likewise the look of brewing storm which had disfigured the Earl's features before he too had betaken himself indoors.

"It would appear so," sighed Petronella sadly, before her heart's delight piped up philosophically:

"Forsooth, I do declare 'twill be the miracle o' the age if the pair o' them e'er see the vicar."

Before anyone could say 'amen' to this young Amelia burst into floods of tears, to her companions' profound concern, and no amount of consoling would becalm her, whilst Nicholas was soundly upbraided for his lack of discretion.

"Gad! Amelia, my love," besought George, distraught with alarm. "Don't take on so! 'Tisn't over yet, they'll come about, you'll see!"

But Amelia shook her inky black ringlets and sobbed all the harder.

"N-No! . . . No," she wailed woefully into her lawn apron as everyone fussed round her. "I-It can't . . . be over . . . b-because it n-never . . . really s-started. Oh, p-poor . . . poor D-Diane!" And she lapsed into a renewed outburst, whilst the three stood helplessly by exchanging bewildered glances.

"What on earth do you mean?" queried Petronella, guiding the grief-stricken girl to a rustic seat, in the hope that she might respond more readily to a fellow female.

"H-He doesn't l-love her!" blubbered Amelia. "He doesn't truly!"

"What? Don't love her?" ejaculated George. "Of course he loves her! Betrothed aren't they?"

"Stap me vitals!" broke in Nicholas incredulously. "You saw 'im, George, didn't ye? Ecod, we all saw 'im! An' whipped out 'is sword and lopped a branch off yonder beech in one fell stroke! I ask ye, is that the action of a rational man?"

"No, but dammit, Nicky, it's Quen we're dealing with," George irately reminded him. "And enraged, to boot!"

"Aye, Quentin in a rage. 'Tis a rare occurrence an' no mistake," accorded Nicholas, wondering what had taken possession of his eldest brother. "Don't see why he should be, after bein' kissed in such fervent fash'n b' the woman he loves, dammim! Could ha' sworn he quite 'njoyed it, though 'twas difficult t' tell who was akissin' who. Rot me, if I han't a likin' to call him out for philanderin' wi' Miss Winstone's 'fections!"

Petronella thought this demonstration of bravado all very well but it was not helping them get to the crux of the matter.

"Amelia?" she probed kindly, sliding a comforting arm about the girl's shoulders. "Is there something you would tell us? Something we ought to know?"

Amelia nodded her head vigorously without raising her face from the haven of the apron.

"B-But Diane made me s-swear . . . not to tell anyone. She s-said if I d-did . . . she'd take m-me away an-and I'd never . . . see m-my dear George again."

A storm of protest greeted this, led by George himself.

"Stuff and nonsense! You'll see me every single day, Amelia, whether you want to or not! And every minute, once we're wed," he declared roundly, giving her and everyone else little say on the issue, "just let anyone try to prevent it!"

"However, you'll be leaving Carnleigh Hall in any case in two days," Petronella pointed out, logically.

"An' y'r cousin's future happiness is at stake," appended Nicholas with fervour, while George replaced Petronella's arm with his own round Amelia's bowed shoulders, accomplishing more with this simple act of affection than all their protestations put together.

Amelia overcame her grief and sat up drying her swollen eyes on George's proferred handkerchief, then raised her blemished face to the three assembled round her.

"I-I hope Diane will forgive me," she faltered, her words punctuated with sniffs. "She swore me to secrecy, but it has all gone wrong, and now, I simply must tell someone." This was readily acknowledged and she went on. "She forbad me to tell anyone that she—that she—"

"Yes?" prompted George, expiring with suspense.

"—that she is not betrothed to your b-brother."

"What!" exploded George and Nicholas in unison.

"N-Not betrothed?" echoed Petronella, perhaps more in the dark than anyone else present.

"No, and never was," completed Amelia, sighing with relief to be finally rid of this terrible burden.

Obviously, George and Nicholas had a deal more to ruminate about this staggering disclosure than had their lady-loves, and a deal more to be incensed about, for they were now close to suspecting the truth of the matter, to wit: that their brother was not, in fact, contracted in marriage to *anyone* and had not the slightest intention of tying the Gordian Knot, at least in the foreseeable future, for he would have scarce encouraged Miss Winstone to act out the farce had he been able to present his true affianced in the flesh.

They had been trapped! Their shrewd brother had cunningly baited his trap—oh, so cunningly, for what better bait could he have used than himself?—into which they had both eagerly leapt in order to evade the threat of the Debtors' Prison. And as they were leaping in to join him in the nuptial snare, he was leaping out to freedom and the gay life. He! The head of the Shadwicks! Obliged by law and the ruling of generations to provide a legitimate son and heir to carry on their noble traditions, for which he was bound to marry. Yet he was escaping whilst they, his brothers, were destined to be prisoners as assuredly as if they had indeed been incarcerated in the Fleet, slamming the door upon them and turning the lock which no key could open— that of wedlock!

"Well! May I be eternally da—" began George, suddenly choking back the red-hot oath on his lips as he remembered the ladies' presence.

"Aye, fie on't, likewise m'self!" snorted Nicholas, his indignation racing neck and neck with George's.

"Come, Nicky!" snapped George, his aggression coming up nicely to the boil. "We've got urgent business to attend to!"

And leaving Amelia to the tender ministrations of Petronella the two brothers set off hot-foot in the direction of the house.

* * *

Lord Carnleigh was in his library, as he was when our narrative began, though not reclining nonchalantly at his desk upon this occasion. For some inexplicable reason he found himself consuming glass upon glass of alcoholic beverage from his Chippendale cabinet in a futile attempt to rid his conscience of, what he could only term a crucifying feeling of guilt, though why he should be thus tormented he was at a loss to understand. Not only had this Miss Diane Winstone been shown every possible consideration during her stay, (indeed, more than any honoured guest that had gone before) and danced attendance upon like the Queen of England, but he himself had humoured her every whim. Tolerated her meddlesome mischief. Suffered his house to be turned inside out and its clockwork-precision organisation thoroughly disrupted So why, why, should he be so plagued? Not to mention her insults. The names she had addressed him by, which he had ne'er thought to hear directed even at a clod-hopping oaf. And his prize Arab stallion would never be the same again. She had transformed it from a well-disciplined docile creature into a wide-eyed stampeding savage. In truth, the sooner she was gone out of his life the better he would be pleased. Or would he? Yes, he would. After all, the idea to pretend to be devoted lovers had been mutual, a pact made between them purely for convenience sake which was due to expire in two days and be resolved quite amicably without ill-feeling on either side. They would bid their adieux and that would be that. There was no possible reason that he could see why either should bear the other a grudge for they had both fulfilled their obligation. So why, in heaven's name, should his conscience continually deny him peace of mind?

Alas! This vital moment when Lord Carnleigh was about to delve into his inner being and plumb the depths of this indefinable emotion, his brothers chose to make their stormy entrance, and in accordance with the first momentous occasion the doors burst back suddenly and George stomped into the room with Nicholas fluttering on his heels.

"We would have words with you, brother Quentin, my lord!" he snapped blisteringly.

"Be good enough to take yourselves off elsewhere," responded his lordship, in no humour at present to stomach a family wrangle as he consumed his fifth glass of potent French brandy. "I have a deal to contemplate."

"Aye, and we're here to give you a deal more to contemplate!" George pointed out acidly. "I repeat, brother Quentin, we would have words with—"

"And I, brother George, would have solitude!" flung back the Earl, taking powerful exception to the other's tone and attitude. "I suggest you better expend your time fawning upon your future brides."

"Ha! As you have fawned upon yours these weeks past?" countered George, gloating to see his arrow hit its mark and nudging Nicholas significantly in the ribs. "We demand an explanation! Do we not, Nicholas? We demand the truth!"

"*Demand*, gentlemen?" queried the Earl, turning to regard them, a dangerous glint in his eye which sent a chill through his youngest brother.

"We-ll," ventured Nicholas, shuffling uneasily, "p'raps we mean—hum—request, eh, George?"

"It matters not a jot what word we use," snorted George, determined not to give an inch. "We are here to ask a question! A simple yea or nay will serve, an it please you to condescend an answer," he felt obliged to add, sensing that Quentin was possessed of a strange humour and not to be trifled with. "It hath been stated by a most reliable person—though under duress, I emphasize—that there is every possibility that you and Di—er—Miss Winstone may not, after all, be—er—be—"

"Affianced!" completed Nicholas bravely. "And if y'r not betrothed to the lady, we'd be exceedin' obleeged to know who y' are betrothed to!"

"Aye, who?" seconded George, fervently.

"It is none of your confounded business!" rasped their brother, his patience wearing thinner. "However, when I do decide to hang the matrimonial millstone about my neck, I guarantee you will be the first to know."

"I knew it! Stap me vitals, I knew it!" cried Nicholas, working up a hysteria.

"But the way you have paid court to her the while?" expostulated George. "You can't mean it was all a sham? All done simply to cozen us?"

"Gadzooks! 'Tan't Christian!" furthered Nicholas.

"I must confess, the entire performance was designed to add conviction to my former promise, namely, that I should return with my intended bride. A chance encounter with Miss Winstone in the village persuaded me that she should fill the role as well as any other—as you yourself later observed, George."

"By Lucifer! You certainly had me convinced!" exclaimed he with vigour. "Especially when you kissed her not half-an-hour agone!"

"Yes, ecod!" burst in Nicholas in ardent support. "As if the whole world were passin' 'em by!"

Strangely enough, this poignant reminder seemed to further disconcert Lord Carnleigh who began to pace the floor in something very akin to agitation.

"I have no desire to discuss the painful business any further, so if you will kindly go—"

"It must be discussed!" insisted George, boldly taking two paces forward.

"Plague take ye, Quen! Ye've always been a gentleman, damme!" vituperated Nicholas. "Ye can't treat her in such shabby fash'n! She loves ye, man!"

The Earl flung Nicholas a look of withering disdain.

"Heaven forfend, I'd be extremely loth to think so, Nicky. Mayhap, you seek to embrace us all in your fantasy world. Methinks you have been duped once again, by Miss Winstone's thespian talent. I must own her a most proficient actress. Faith, there were times when she almost had me convinced."

"Acting, you term it?" rejoined George, about to burst with exasperation. "When she lies abovestairs at this very moment, her heart torn asunder with anguish?"

The Earl shrugged nonchalantly. "She is also adept at throwing the vapours."

"'S death! For a man o' perception y're oft-times deuced obtuse, Quentin," remarked Nicholas, relinquishing the battle in despair.

"Forgive me, Nicky," bowed his lordship with a

sneer. "But on this occasion, I'm afraid, the responsibility must rest with the brandy."

"But you can't be indifferent to her, Quentin! You can't!" George went on, refusing to give up. "The way you kissed her out there, 'fore gad, I've never witnessed anything like it! And don't tell me it was nought but an act for our benefit because you and she were more taken aback than we—that so, Nicky?"

"Me life on't!" vowed Nicholas with equal fervour.

"My feelings are my own personal concern!" the Earl rebuffed them harshly, swinging back to the cabinet, unable to withstand their accusations. "I'll thank you both to cease interfering!"

"Aye, you're usually a clever devil at hiding your feelings, Quentin," George could not resist informing him. "But this time you're hiding them from no one but yourself!"

"Amen t' that!" appended Nicholas.

"Furthermore, yours aren't the only feelings to be considered!"

The Earl put down the glass and abandoned the wine-cabinet to stroll over to the doors where he positioned himself, his back against the panelling, a manoeuvre which did not occasion remark, as yet. Thus he stood, inhaling deeply, steadily regarding his problem brothers, a look loaded with suspicion, almost sinister, though when he spake his voice was quite casual.

"Doth not it seem somewhat curious that a female of Miss Winstone's breeding and sound moral precepts should choose to deliberately act the lie? And whilst you come thus accusing me, mayhap, the solution to the whole sordid mystery lies within your two selves?"

George did not care for this turn of conversation and

was about to escape, alas, to find the only way out barred by his elder brother.

"Er—well, as we've no more to say on the subject, Quentin, we'll leave you in peace," he announced, edging Nicholas to little purpose in the direction of the doors.

"Having stirred up this hornets' nest, you will stay to suffer the consequences and hear me out, and remember the while, that you brought it upon yourselves!"

As Nicholas fought valiantly to preserve his calm, George shuffled uncomfortably from foot to foot, though prepared to brazen it all out for the problem was as yet a molehill. Granted, Quentin was in no mood to withstand undue provocation but if Nicky would hold his tongue and let him handle the fomenting situation then there was every chance that the day might be saved, and their hides along with it.

"To resume," the Earl went on with equanimity. "Why, think you, should she deem it necessary to pronounce herself as my future bride?"

"Fie on ye! 'Twas y'rself pronounced her t' be such," contradicted Nicholas with toss of fair curls.

"Alas no, Nicholas," corrected the Earl, condescendingly. "For the origin of the misconception you must cast your memory back prior to my advent, for long ere I abandoned ship Miss Winstone had established herself as my affianced. Now why, I find myself asking? Perchance for some ulterior motive, like personal gain? No, I think not. This, her conscience and sense of propriety would certainly not allow."

The Earl paused, furtively surveying the guilty pair through his long dark lashes, shrewdly biding his time, observing with an air of satisfaction that Nicholas was weaking visibly.

"I nurture more than a faint suspicion that her reason may have been prompted by some basic animal instinct, possibly fear—"

A loud gasp issued from Nicholas.

"—for her welfare, or that of her young cousin. Mayhap, she found herself cornered and was driven to making the admission against her will, for protection?"

An inarticulate squeak now erupted from Nicholas whilst George scowled thunderously, unamused at the way they were being manipulated into position like puppets by their brother, yet were unable to do much about it.

"Protection against what, exactly?" he snapped, appreciating for the first time how Diane Winstone had felt when cornered in similar fashion.

"Perchance *you* would deign to enlighten *me*, George?" No, on second thoughts he would gain nothing from George, and so the Earl turned his attention to the quivering Nicholas. Yes, Nicholas was quite ready to capitulate. "Or you, Nicky? Surely having earned an enviable reputation with the sex it does not stretch the imagination beyond the boundaries of credibility to envisage you seducing two such young ladies against their will—"

"No! Gad! 'Fore heaven, I-I swear! I ne'er laid a digit on 'em, on oath! And Miss Winstone herself, if ye won't take me sacred word! She'll tell ye—"

"Stow your gab, you clacking fool!" barked George lest Nicholas expose all.

"No! Shan't! 'Twasn't my idea! Told ye no good would come of it but ye wouldn't listen! Insisted on havin' y'r accurst way!"

"You're in it as deep as I am!" bellowed George,

turning a colourful apoplectic-purple. "Who carried 'em off in the first place?"

"I didn't! I swear, Quentin, 'pon m' life! 'Twasn't like that! Miss Winstone—sh-she accosted me—her cousin had the sickness, the ague! She begged me to take the two of 'em—"

"To the next inn," cut in George with a snarl of contempt. "And you brought them here instead, which, in the eyes of the law, is brazen-faced abduction!"

"Devil take ye for a foul-mouthed lyin' blackguard! 'Twas *your* suggest'n t' carry off an heiress and hold her t' ransom!"

"Because *you* wouldn't wed her!"

"Ye know deuced well she wouldn't have me! And ye vowed on gospel oath if she refused ye'd let her go free and ye recanted y'r word and wanted t' keep 'em both prisoners!"

As the echo of Nicholas's hysterical screech wailed into obscurity silence blanketed the atmosphere, for apart from having no apt requital to this, George could not see much purpose in continuing to protest his innocence when Quentin was already in possession of the facts, and so abundantly aware of his guilt. All was finally revealed. There was obviously nothing left to do but mutter imprecations to heaven and brace himself to receive the full blast of his elder brother's wrath which, though he kept his gaze riveted to the floor, he could sense was building up to cataclysmic proportions.

But no explosion came, to George's speechless amazement, for the Earl had managed—though one might marvel precisely how—to suppress his fury. Nevertheless, it was some appreciable time before he could trust himself to speak, and when he did, his voice bore evidence of the emotional battle consuming him.

"Have either of you anything further to divulge? Or is this the sum total of your atrocities?"

"S-Sum total," affirmed George, barely audibly.

Again the excruciating silence descended as the Earl crossed from the doors to the windows, as if unable to bear the sight of his brothers any longer.

"Had I cherished any . . . profound feeling . . . for Miss Winstone," he ventured hoarsely, gazing out upon the vista of his estate, "you doubtless appreciate that this confession would have . . . dealt a . . . a death blow?"

This gave the guilty pair food for thought, wondering if this was their brother's ambiguous way of telling them that the havoc they had wrought with their impetuous actions ran much deeper than they were wont to think. In their feverish concern for their own future happiness, had they inadvertently sacrificed his?

"How?" George managed to utter, to wait several seconds ere his lordship responded.

"How, George?" he murmured from a distant plain. "Simply because she would never believe my feeling to be genuine, and would naturally assume me to be offering myself as some kind of compensation for the outrage she has been accorded."

For the first time in his life George sensed the true meaning of remorse, a bitter remorse! A remorse which was urging him to cast himself bodily at Quentin's feet and crave his forgiveness. And whereas he had never wept in his entire years—and was certainly not going to do so now!—it did not prevent a huge lump the size of a duck's egg mounting in his throat, which had never happened before. Indeed, the Earl could not have inflicted greater punishment on his brothers had he implemented his former threat and dragged them below to the dungeons and subjected them to the agonies of every instrument of torture in his collection.

"I-I beg forgiveness, Quentin," petitioned George at length, now of reformed character. "I-I had no idea that . . . i-if there is anything I can do to atone . . ."

"Aye, likewise ap-apologies, Quenting," faltered Nicholas timorously, as much at a loss as George who, suddenly aware of a sense of duty and responsibility as next in line, took four paces forward to confront the Earl and raised his right hand aloft.

"Quentin, brother, my lord. We do hereby solemnly vow on sacred oath to do all in our power to undo the wrong we have done, and not rest in our earnest endeavours until Miss Wins—"

"No!" the Earl cried out, his anger flaring anew as he rounded on them from the window. "You will leave well alone! By the saints, you cannot begin to comprehend the full extent of the damage you have caused, let alone undo it! Next time you will not find me quite so charitable!" He paused, breathing deeply to regain command of himself, and when he had done so, continued in calmer tone. "You have my permission to approach Miss Winstone on your bended knees and beseech her forgiveness for your deplorable conduct, and for no other reason. Is that understood?"

This met with sullen nods and mumbled acknowledgements, George suddenly conscious that he had a prodigious amount of apologising to do to Miss Winstone, now recalling that the night of her arrival had not been the only occasion upon which he had threatened her person. Neither had he yet summoned sufficient courage to thank her for saving Nicky's life.

Dubiously satisfied, Lord Carnleigh turned back to the window.

" 'Tis fortunate, is it not, that I do not happen to cherish any such feeling for the lady?" he flung over his shoulder with an admirable attempt at his customary nonchalance. "And that I emerge from the encounter virtually unscathed? Faith, methinks I am to be envied, sustaining nought more grievous than a crushing blow to my pride at having to suffer the ultimate in humiliation."

Fourteen

———•———

George, it may be said, had not the slightest intention of allowing his elder brother to wallow to his heart's content in his martyrdom. He adamantly refused to sit back and watch him drink himself into an early grave, which now seemed to be his one ambition in life.

Consequently, it was not long before the embryo of a brilliant counter-plan was shaping in the back of George's mind, designed to open Quentin's eyes to the truth staring him starkly in the face yet which he stubbornly refused to acknowledge.

George could scarce contain his excitement and chortled and hugged himself with glee ·as he gradually pieced his strategem together. Granted, he would need the full cooperation of Nicky which could prove a stumbling-block, but only a minor one, for when he discovered the major part he was to play in saving Quentin's soul from perdition, he would rally wholeheartedly to the cause.

Not until his ruse was complete in every detail did George undertake to confide the whole to Nicholas who deemed it an excellent scheme—until he discovered that not only was he expected to run the gauntlet of Quentin's wrath in the process, but risk losing Petronella irretrievably—when he demurred most vociferously. Anticipating this, George was quick to reassure him that contrary to evoking their brother's wrath he would, in fact, merit his undying gratitude when all was revealed and he realised the tremendous service Nicholas had done him, for which he would no doubt recompense him befittingly—though whether it would be good or ill George did not choose to enlarge upon. Furthermore, there was not the slightest chance of losing his fair Petronella for George himself would take her into his strict confidence once Nicholas was off on his imperative mission. Nicholas eventually, though reluctantly, agreed, and only on the rigid condition that George made absolutely certain to explain everything to Petronella so that there should be no misunderstanding.

But the wily George had no intention whatsoever of making Petronella as wise as himself, for the role he had destined for her demanded that she, more than any other, give a wholly convincing performance in order to outwit his uncommonly astute, and equally suspicious, elder brother. Therefore, it was essential that Petronella's reaction be quite, quite, genuine, and to this end it were better that she remain in complete ignorance.

Meanwhile, contrary to common assumption, Diane was not still submerged in her grief during these machinations. Having wept her eyes dry again into her pillow she was now striving to overcome her disillusionment and broken heart, though certain she would never overcome the terrible humiliation of having revealed her innermost feelings to her host in that fatal kiss which would brand her soul for all time. In these calamitous circumstances she could not bring herself to confront him again, and so had arrived at the momentous decision that it would be better for all concerned if she and Amelia secretly packed their effects and stole away by way of the servants stair, to be well *en route* to Thatcham before they were even missed. Of course, she would need to confide the whole to George for she doubted prodigiously if Amelia could be prevailed upon to leave at all unless she were granted permission and time to bid her fond *au revoirs*.

Strangely enough, the proposal to leave two days earlier than arranged did not meet with the display of tantrums and perversity from Amelia that Diane had anticipated. To her astonishment, her cousin actually seemed delighted at the news and even laughed about it! Moreover, George seemed disposed to treat the sad departure with the same flippancy, and took it upon himsef to see that all the clandestine arrangements were put into effect as quickly and quietly as possible, as if more anxious than they for them to be gone. However, she did consider he was to be admired at the way in which he organised everything right down to most minor detail, even bethinking to command the coach and four to stand well out of sight of the house lest they be discovered, particularly as it was still broad daylight.

Everything went according to plan, and as it was approaching three o'clock Diane found herself mounting the coach steps to await Amelia—who was bidding her last minute farewells to George—and sinking back with heavy-laden heart into the blue plush upholstery of the luxurious conveyance. Nevertheless, she was thankful that everything had happened so swiftly that she had not had time to repine nor fully appreciate her loss.

Eventually, the last piece of baggage was hoisted on to the box as Amelia arrived, Diane relieved to note that she had sensibly taken the necessary precautions against catching a possible chill and was well wrapped, for despite the agreeable weather it was to be remembered that she was not long risen from a sick-bed.

It was not until they were well under way and Carnleigh Hall growing smaller and smaller on the horizon that Diane suffered her first pangs of regret, for despite her grim determination not to look back she could not resist flashing the occasional glance at the great house wherein lodged the man to whom she had eternally relinquished her heart, the only man she could ever love in the whole world yet who could not, because of an overdose of pride and his gruelling self-discipline, bring himself to cede to the dictates of his heart.

He had loved her! For one brief raptuorous moment he had actually loved her! Had lowered his impregnable guard and permitted that tender, yet passionate emotion to break through, an experience she would never forget and which she would never experience again.

She swallowed hard, trying to overcome her mounting despair and the tears which followed close behind. Several times she strove bravely to banish all thought of the past two months from her mind but found it impossible, especially when Amelia whimpered and sniffled into her handkerchief at frequent intervals, obviously in sudden harsh appreciation that she was cruelly parted from her George, as she shrank back within the capacious hood of her capuchin, shielding her misery from the world.

Howbeit, it was at this point that Diane remarked something passing strange, to wit, a strand of long silken hair, not of Amelia's thick black as one might expect, but of a distinctive fair colour, and as fine as gossamer. Immediately, she leaned forward the better to examine the incongruity, loth to add to her burden of wretchedness by acknowledging the suspicions already surging to the fore.

"A-Amelia?" she ventured cautiously, straining her eyes to peer inside the hood which availed her nought for Amelia sank her face deeper still into her handkerchief and wailed the harder until Diane whisked off the offending hood in one swift movement to reveal—a stricken Nicholas.

For fully half a minute each stared aghast at the other before Diane collapsed onto the seat with a gasp of utter defeat.

"Oh no, Nicholas," she groaned, as if this were the ultimate test of her endurance. "Not another abduction!"

"Er—no, ma'am, 'tis meant t' be an elopement—d-deuced sorry if I startled ye," he explained, cowering into his corner as if half-suspecting she might run rampant and do him bodily harm. "D-Don't be angry, ma'am, I beg ye. Not my fault, I swear! 'Twas George's idea t' do ye a service by makin' Quentin wild wi' jealousy!" he enlarged, waxing enthusiastic, trusting the lady would follow suit. "Open his eyes and realise that he truly loves ye an' wants ye for his bride after all! George planned it. Thought I'd prove the better at elopin' with ye due t' Quentin appreciatin' me repute wi' the ladies—hum—'fore I gave me heart t' Petronella, o' course."

But Diane's despair did not transform miraculously into enthusiasm. Instead, it blended into a mixture of horror, anger and acute nausea as she strained back against the cushions, eyes closed, battling vainly to suppress the repugnant feeling and re-establish her self-possession. To suffer this on top of all else was the final blow to her self-respect, her whole future, her ability to start life anew, for no matter where she went or whom she met she would never be able to rid herself of the feeling that everyone was pointing a finger of scorn at her, ridiculing her for what she was and what she had presumptuously aspired to be. The whole village would buzz of it by the morrow, that she had been betrothed to Lord Carnleigh who had spurned her, and so she had sought to spite him by eloping with his brother. And the ripples from such a scandal soon spread far and wide.

But the worst pain of all generated from the excruciating embarrassment which would be hers if the Earl should come galloping to her rescue—as was the obvious intention behind the plan—and which would prove absolutely nothing for such action was no more than any gentleman of honour would take to protect a lady's reputation. On the other hand, it would be equally humiliating if he did not chance to come at all. Evidently, George and Nicholas had not paused to weigh these possibilities, and that their scheme—though admirable upon the stage and in theory—might have tragic consequences. But try as she might, she simply could not reproach them for what they were doing for she was fully aware that at heart the two nurtured the very best intentions, and deemed themselves to be assisting in Cupid's cause.

It was some considerable while ere Diane could summon the will to sweep aside the havoc thus wrought and centre her thoughts upon some counter-plot, rallying herself with the idea that all might not yet be lost. True, they had been travelling at a goodly pace for almost an hour, but even so, if they turned back at once it was possible that they might arrive at Carnleigh Hall before the Earl discovered their absence and accordingly avert disaster.

With this in mind she suddenly sat up erect to pierce Nicholas with a determined eye. Nicholas bolted upright too as if ready to lend his undying support to anything she had a mind to propose—anything, that was, *except* returning to Carnleigh.

"Nicholas, we must turn back at once!" she declared in a tone that would brook no refusal, preparing to hail the coachman on the box.

"No! No! N-Not that! We can't!" he whined, his refined features distorted with abject horror as he plucked anxiously at the rosebuds adorning his muslin gown. "Ecod! I durst not! George would kill me!"

"And if George doesn't, I will!" she responded, preparing to suit action to words by relieving the holster by the door of its Italian flintlock pistol and pointing it in Nicky's direction.

Nicholas recoiled into the seat, his knees clutched to his chin.

"Gadswoons, n-not violence! P-Please . . . dislike it intens'ly! W-Will do as ye suggest—anythin'—but I beg o' ye t' put the demmed thing back!"

Despite the grave situation Diane could not forgo a wan smile as she replaced the pistol. After all, how could Nicholas know that she would choose to suffer her humiliation at the hands of his elder brother rather than harm him in any way? Or that the pistol in question was not even primed?

Fifteen

Meanwhile, at Carnleigh Hall, Lord Carnleigh, the guileless and unsuspecting hero of the piece, was seated in his dressing-room shrouded in a cloud of blackest humour, striving against the tremendous odds of semi-intoxication to conduct his toilet, though ably assisted by two flunkeys, his valet de chambre, friseur, and regular collection of cosmetics, perfumes and patch-boxes.

The ritual was blanketed in silence, the valet and friseur having long since abandoned their endeavours to offer helpful suggestions in the most obsequious manner to their master who repeatedly and curtly gestured them to hold their piece. Indeed, the two—along with everyone else in the Carnleigh service—were in something of a dilemma as to how to deal with my lord's sudden attack of spleen, for he had never been known to suffer with such before, consequently, no one was able to prescribe an antidote.

Here, a scratch sounded upon the door of the closet, to reveal Jenkins who entered with the customary low bow, and looking a trifle more than anxious.

"Well, Jenkins?" demanded the Earl, resenting the menial's intrusion at this present time.

"A gentleman belowstairs to wait upon your lordship," he ventured uncertainly. "Er—a rather elderly gentleman—bewhiskered, my lord, c-comes in great haste on a matter of some urgency—"

"His name?" broke in his master impatiently, in the delicate process of positioning a patch upon his left cheekbone.

The head footman gave an embarrassed cough.

"Er—refuses to divulge it, m' lord," appending hurriedly, "—but he seems to be of good stock, though a little out of humour, perhaps."

The Earl hesitated, blinking his eyes to clear his vision before embarking upon his third attempt to place the patch.

"Where is he?"

"In the Porcelain Room, the Music Salon, and the Library, my lord," responded Jenkins, without a flicker of a muscle.

"All at once?" exclaimed his master, flinging away the offending patch in despair.

"The gentleman appears to be somewhat agitated, my lord, and—er—moves about a deal—"

"Kindly request him to establish himself in the Main Drawing-room. I'll see him directly," interjected the Earl, taking up the haresfoot as Jenkins disappeared with a final bow.

Lord Carnleigh anon relinquished the haresfoot, gave a cursory glance at his fingernails, and rose from his dresser to receive his coat of dove-grey damask generously laced with silver, complimenting the impeccable whiteness of his lace ruffles and silk gold-clocked stockings.

The three-inch heels of his gold-buckled shoes tapped out an impatient rhythm as he descended the Grand Staircase and crossed the expanse of hall to the

Drawing-room where liveried footmen sprang to open the doors.

Howbeit, barely had the Earl over-stepped the threshold when a rather rotund figure clad in mulberry superfine came blustering up, his visage—which contended narrowly with the hue of his coat—topped by a liberally powdered campaign wig and bordered on each side by incongruous iron-grey whiskers.

"My Lord Carnleigh?" he queried gruffly.

The Earl returned the other's abrupt bow.

"At your service—er—alas, 'twould seem you have the advantage of me—"

"Haw! Won't mince matters," he blustered on, dispensing with the irksome formality of introducing himself. "Have reason to believe ye have me daughter here, sir, y'r lordship, and I'll thank ye to hand her over to me at once. I've travelled a tidy distance, and suffered a number o' setbacks, nonetheless, here I am, cursed b' shortness o' breath and temper so if ye'll just have her fetched we'll take ourselves off and no more said on't."

"Your daughter?" prompted the Earl, finally able to insert a word despite the gentleman's acclaimed breathlessness. "Your name is perchance Winstone? Ah, no! I recall the sire of that particular young lady departed this life some years agone. Hm-m, Reynolds, then?"

"Reynolds? It most certainly is not, sir! And I'd give me left eye-ball to know just how many daughters ye've got secreted about the place!"

"At the last count—two, I fancy," returned the Earl with infuriating candour, more adept at suppressing his ill-humour than his guest. "A Winstone, and a Reynolds. But, neither is yours, you say? Your name, you are certain, is not Reynolds?"

The gentleman puffed up his cheeks like an over-ripe tomato ready to burst its skin.

"I'll have ye know, sirrah, that I am Sir Jason Wilchards, o' Warmley Manor, and as good as any 'curst aristocrat, aye, despite y'r fine Rembrandts and Titians, and never-ending line o' ancestors who no doubt wasted th'r substance in riotous livin' like all the rest!"

This did nought to improve my lord's mood. The day was certainly not proving to be one of his best and to culminate in this unexpected visit from Sir Jason Wilchards, of all unlikely people, which he would willingly have forgone, was more than flesh and blood could stand.

"I assure you, Sir Jason," responded the Earl in thinly veiled contempt, directing the visitor to a chair large enough to accommodate his ample person, "that the works of art displayed about you and the shortcomings of my ancestors were never intended to impress your goodself nor anyone else, but to give pleasure to the Shadwick family. Howbeit, I'm sure you did not journey hither solely to pass judgement upon my home and forebears?"

The gibe exacerbated Sir Jason's annoyance as he was feeling uncomfortably out of place in his noble surroundings even though he could boast a shilling or two himself, and secretly cherished the idea of having an 'accurst aristocrat' for a son-in law. Indeed, to his further annoyance, he suddenly became conscious of the fact that his wig which he had nurtured with tender care from the '45 Rebellion, was woefully out of mode, and he was set wondering why, as it had never bothered him before, he should now be seized with the irresistible urge to snatch it from his bald pate and hurl it out of the window.

"Damme, no sir!" he fumed. "I want my daughter, and in the same virtuous condition she came here! And I do not quit this house until I get her!"

In corroboration with this he plumped his great bulk down upon the formentioned chair, where he seemed determined to remain till the crack of doom.

"Your daughter—er—Wilchards . . ." reflected the Earl, certain he had heard the name of late. "You must excuse me, I have but recently returned from Italy and am not yet fully conversant with the sequence of events."

Sir Jason repaid this with a snort of contempt.

"She fancies herself in love with a young rake of a brother o' yourn."

"Might I enquire which brother you refer to?"

"Wh-Which one!" spluttered his guest. "Hang me, sir! How many rakes number in your family when they're all at home?"

"Er—three, if you choose to include myself," obliged my lord. "However, I harbour more than a faint suspicion that you refer to Nicholas, the youngest ne-er-do-well, who boasts an eye for the sex."

"By gad, sirrah! There seems little to choose 'twixt ye!"

The Earl turned to view him awhile as if trying to determine if he were being flattered or no, his mind suddenly clearing as he recalled one of Miss Winstone's earlier conversations.

"Ah, Petronella, is it not?"

"If ye mean m' daughter's name, yes!" barked his visitor. "And if ye've nothing further to say, I'll take her and go!"

"Alas, I doubt if 'tis so simply resolved," replied the Earl, hailing a lackey to furnish himself and his guest with some liquid refreshment. "To my knowledge, I have no one bearing such a name 'neath my roof."

" 'S blood! I don't believe it!" exploded Sir Jason anew. "I refuse to accept it! I shan't——"

"In which case, you have my permission to search the entire house."

"Blast it! A house this size? 'Twould take from now till Christmastide! And whilst I'm busy searching one wing the little minx will be evading me in another!"

"You appear to be quite certain that she is here?"

"Bound to be! Came to elope with this reprobate brother o' yourn."

"Which may indicate that they have already eloped," observed the Earl, none too helpfully.

As the footman served the wine at this point, the door flew open and the Earl glanced up to see hastening towards him none other than Nicky's chambermaid, in a state of such frantic alarm that she did not glance to right nor left—nor even realise that the Earl was entertaining anyone, let alone her own father.

"Oh, my lord! My lord! F-Forgive me, but I bring t-terrible news!" she cried, wild with anxiety, the tears glistening on her golden lashes and about to rain down her cheeks at any moment. "It-It's Nicholas! He's——"

"Petronella!" spluttered Sir Jason over a mouthful of wine.

"Father!" gasped she in horror.

"Oh lud!" came the unmistakable voice of George from the region of the keyhole in one of the doors.

"Well, sirrah!" Sir Jason rounded on his lordship—who could only return a look of mute astonishment. "D-ye still deny ye have me daughter here?"

"This?—is your daughter?" questioned the Earl,

subjecting Petronella to closer scrutiny. "In my employ as a chambermaid?"

Sir Jason turned as red as a turkey-cock as he sought to explain the irregularity.

"Haw! Sure to be some—hum—reasonable explanation," stammered he doubtfully, viewing his daughter's distraught state with some concern.

"Yes! Yes! There is, father! But I haven't time to explain it all now! We must hurry! Please, my lord!" she turned to petition the Earl, tears now descending freely down her face. "I-I implore you . . ."

"Faith, child! What's amiss?" he queried, offering his silk monogrammed handkerchief as Sir Jason rallied round her in a paternal manner.

"N-Nicholas . . ." she sobbed. "H-He's eloped!"

"He's *what?*" echoed the gentlemen in unison.

"Eloped! Gone! Oh, Lord Carnleigh, you must do something quickly! Someone must overtake them before nightfall or all will be truly lost! Sh-She will be quite undone! Ruined! Her reputation in shreds with no hope of future employment!"—sob—"And Nicholas—m-my Nicholas—"—sob—"l-lost to me f-for ever!"

Convulsed with grief, Petronella collapsed upon her father's broad shoulder, burying her face from view.

"Well, dammit! That can be no bad thing by all accounts!" declared Sir Jason roundly. "A regular Don Juan, an' no mistake! P'raps ye'll hearken to y'r father in future, Mistress Wayward. Saved ye in the nick o' time!"

This was too much for Petronella. It was more than she could bear to have her father think further ill of Nicholas, the man she still loved with all her heart no matter what he had done, for whatever it was she was sure he would be able to explain it all away.

"Oh no, father! Y-You're wrong!" she cried heart-broken. "H-He isn't like that at all! He's wonderful! The most wonderful man in the whole world! I love him with all my heart and could never love nor wed any other! P-Please, father, I can't bear you to think ill of my dearest Nicky . . ."

Before his own eyes the Earl now witnessed a miracle—of the female of the human species at work, utilizing every wile and strategem known to her sex to inveigle the male to her way. What mere mortal could possibly withstand such witchery of appeal? Certainly not Sir Jason Wilchards who was soon reduced from a presumptuous over-bearing blusterer to a quivering mass of fatherly solicitude, ready to grant his daughter all it was in his power to give as he caressed her golden child-like head with a tender hand which trembled with affection, likewise his voice.

"And ye shall have him, child, never fear. I give ye m' word—hum—if his lordship here will give his?"

What could the Earl do but smile and bow his acknowledgement with all the aplomb at his command, secretly delighted with the match.

"That will not be necessary, Sir Jason," he observed graciously. "Nicholas has long gained his majority."

Petronella raised up her tear-streaked face to her father and forced a weak smile.

"Y-You will not p-press me . . to w-wed Lord P-Pottle, father?"

"Nay, child," beamed Sir Jason, hugging her like a great playful bear. "Never partic'larly cared for the f'low, t' be honest, though y'r mother did."

"I'm sure you will like Nicholas, father. He would never ever do anything wicked, really. I am certain he doesn't mean to go through with this elopement—"

"Oh yes he does!" burst in George at this point to prevent Petronella unwittingly ruining his whole meticulous scheme. "Been planning it for weeks, he has! Stake my soul on't!—er—good den to you, Sir Jason! George Shadwick at your service, sir!" he deemed it proper to introduce himself. "Professed love for Miss Wilchards here simply to divert attention away from the true object of his heart, Miss Winstone! Gad! Couldn't keep his orbs off her! Spied on her every minute he had! Sent her gifts, and wrote her odes, aye—sheaves of 'em!"

"No! No! Never! It's not true! He's lying!" screamed Petronella anew, unaware that she was playing right into George's trap and adding authenticity to her role.

"Yes Yes! 'Tis true! All perfectly true! May I be stricken with plague if I speak aught but the pure unadulterated truth!" swore he recklessly.

"Take care lest you be stricken dead, George Shadwick, for the sinful way you defile your own sweet brother!" warned Petronella, venomously.

Loth to tempt Providence any further, George held his peace, which opportunity the Earl took to intervene.

"Are you endeavouring to tell us that Miss Winstone has eloped with Nicholas—of her own volition?" he enquired sceptically.

"No, dammit!—er—your pardon, ma'am," exclaimed George in exasperation. "By force! Against her will! Carried her off, he has, to some outlandish spot intending to seduce her at his pleasure, the mealymouthed blackguard!" he went on, obliged to overact his part for his suspicious brother was taking a deal of convincing. "Gad! What ghastly fate for sweet blooming damsel in such dire distress! Sink me, if I didn't hear her cry out for aid—"

"Then why did you not hie hence to her aid, craven?" challenged Petronella cuttingly.

"Who dares to name my dearest George, craven?" came Amelia's high-pitched petulant voice from the doorway.

"Look, Quentin! See? Here's Amelia!"

The Earl followed his indication with an indifferent eye.

"Well?" he drawled. "Is that meant to prove something?"

"Is it not proof enough that Miss Winstone has gone off with Nicky? Everyone else is here assembled!" emphasized George, overjoyed to see his brother summon a footman to whom he murmured some instructions and who then hastened away.

"That does not signify, George! It still does not give anyone the right to term you craven," declared the object of his heart, swishing into the room in her Parisian creation of cream painted silk and lace, to curtsy to the company and be introduced to Sir Jason.

"Neither does it signify that Miss Winstone went under duress," observed his brother, narrowly surveying him.

"Oh but it does, my lord!—if you'll forgive me intruding," broke in Amelia in ardent support of George, her wide hazel eyes gazing up into the Earl's stern countenance with cherub-like innocence. "I witnessed the dastardly deed myself, from the window of my boudoir! And saw Nicholas laying violent hands upon my p-poor Diane—forcing her most brutally into the coach, and holding a pistol to her head! He even tried to—"

"Yes, well—er—no matter, Amelia," interrupted George hastily, before his lady went too far in her eagerness to impress, for he was anxious to hold Quentin's interest which was wavering on the brink of credibility. "Anywise, she wasn't calling for me to come to her aid, but you, Quentin! Quentin! Quentin! Save me, my heart's own true love!"—cough—"or—hum—words to such effect. I vow I thought I was dreaming it all for I lay composing myself before dinner and dozed a little, but upon waking, discovered it all, alack, tragically true."

"By gad! What a catastrophic business!" muttered Sir Jason, wondering how he should ever reconcile himself to having this Nicholas Shadwick for a son-in-law.

"But it's not true! It's not!" cried out Petronella in anguish. "They're both lying quite shamefully! Can't you see? Nicholas could *never* behave in this manner!"

George glanced up of a sudden to find his elder brother positioned at uncomfortably close quarters, looking down on him with what he could only term a murderous glint in his implacable gaze, enough to strike fear into the most redoubtable heart, let alone the cowardly one of George.

"Do you solemnly swear upon your very life and before God that you had no part in this? That every single word you speak is the sacred incontestable truth?" he hissed menacingly, his voice so soft it was barely audible—even to George.

"A-As h-heaven is my w-witness," stammered the latter, loth to tempt Providence yet again with this blatant lie, but cornered as he was betwixt heaven and his brother he had little choice, and if he were obliged to suffer the wrath of one, he would rather it were that of heaven!

"My love, you tremble," exclaimed Amelia, blinking wide-eyed at him in concern. "You have taken a chill."

"No, 'tis nought to fuss about. Mayhap I have contracted the pox and will expire ere midnight," gasped George, hopefully, before beseeching his brother anew—primarily to divert suspicion from himself. "Hang me, Quentin, you must do something! Can't let Miss Winstone languish unprotected! You know Nicky's appetite for the sex, dammit, and how they fall victim to his charms like ripe plums off a tree when he sets to work! Rally yourself, man! Do the decent thing for once in your life! Gird on your armour like your deuced ancestors in days of yore, and go fight for a maiden's honour, confound you! Armour aplenty in the Armoury—pikes, halberds, crossbows, cutlasses, battle-axes—"

"Rot me! Is't one man he's to face or a veritable regiment?" cut in Sir Jason.

"Hm-m," quoth George, with a sheepish glance all round. "Shouldn't hesitate to go myself but I'm no flash swordsman! Not like you, Quentin. By Jingo! Heard it said that Quentin was born sword in hand!" he enlightened the company with a weak laugh, in which no one felt inclined to join.

"Sword!" shrieked Petronella, dealing a death-blow to his quip. "N-Not for my Nicky?"

"Why not?" countered George, goading poor Petronella into giving the most brilliant performance in history. " 'Tis scarce two hours since Nicholas threw down the gauntlet at Quentin's feet!—or where they'd been, anyway! Threatened to call you out, Quen, for philandering with Miss Winstone's affections. His exact words, eh, Amelia? Aye, before witnesses, to boot!"

As expected, Amelia was not slow to leap to her beloved George's defence.

"I swear on my honour, your lordship, that every word George speaks is perfectly true. I was one of the witnesses, and so was Petronella!" she added smugly.

The Earl turned slowly to Petronella who stood clinging for protection to her father's right arm.

"So you deny this, Miss Wilchards?" he queried of her, quietly.

A breathless hush fell all round during which the emotional battle being waged within the girl could almost be heard, before she answered.

"N-No, my lord . . . that I cannot deny. But he didn't mean it! I swear he didn't! Oh, Lord Carnleigh, y-you aren't going to k-kill him? Your own dear brother?" she cried after the Earl as he turned away without further comment. "No! You shan't! I won't let you!" she went on waxing hysterical. "Father! Stop them!"

As Sir Jason tried to calm his daughter, the footman returned to whisper in confidence to his master, evidently confirming George's tale to the extent of the two rooms being vacated by the guilty pair with all the lady's baggage gone, and the coach and four having been seen by an ostler as it bowled down the driveway, the ostler assuming it to be carrying the two young ladies to Thatcham and so not regarding it as strange.

Naturally, George was not slow to cock an ear to this, and fairly danced with joy to see his brother quit the room without further ado, dutifully followed by the lackey.

His plan was into effect! Quentin had taken the bait!

All he had to do now was reassure Petronella that all would be well, that Quentin would not harm a hair of Nicky's sweet head—but not yet awhile . . . not until his brother was well on his way. No, Quentin could never bring himself to harm the baby of the family! Nor even pink him in his pride! And to think he might venture actually to kill him, well, it was just too ridiculous to contemplate.

However, when Lord Carnleigh eventually reappeared equipped for the road in doeskin breeches, thigh-length riding boots, and claret riding-coat, George was seized with the first pangs of misgiving to espy hanging ominously by his side, not the customary light dress sword, but his gold-hilted, deadly-looking, full length rapier.

Sixteen

———◆———

As Lord Carnleigh prepared to mount his horse, his damsel—purportedly in distress—was rumbling into the yard of The Jingling Jester with her escort, two miles out of Islington, the equipage commanding sufficient attention for two ostlers to leap to the horses' heads and another to let down the steps that the two fine ladies might alight, for which services they would no doubt be handsomely recompensed. A meagre penny apiece was all Nicholas saw fit to bestow before accompanying Miss Winstone over the dusty cobbles and up the shallow stone steps into the modest hostelry, doing his level best to conceal himself—despite his dazzling butter-coloured gown and purple cloak—behind her dignified person.

Once inside, the amply proportioned innkeeper adorned in white apron and grizzled scratch wig came rolling up with nautical gait, rubbing his spatulate hands and bowing as low as his huge abdomen would allow, to enquire the pleasure of his honoured guests. It was perhaps unfortunate that Nicholas momentarily forgot himself by calling out with his customary arrogance for a private room and repast that the lady might refresh and compose herself ere she resumed her journey, prompting mine host to query, with due respect, which lady he was referring to as he could see two despite the fact that he was completely sober.

Nicholas humbly retired within his cloak, screening his blushes from view whilst Diane assumed command of the situation, and before long they were being led up a somewhat precarious wooden stair by a rosy-cheeked serving wench to the inn's most luxurious room which was complete with warped table, three chairs, sparsely covered bed and dresser with cracked mirror-stand, leaving the innkeeper to gaze after the incongruous pair with eyes shrewdly narrowed.

A broad grin was soon over-spreading his full-blown visage as he detected beneath the façade all the obvious signs of a runaway couple. Indeed, he had not plied his business on this initial stretch of the Great North Road without observing the peculiarities of certain of his patrons, and how exceedingly popular his inn was become since the Marriage Act was passed six years agone, proclaiming the Fleet marriages and other clandestine ceremonies as unlawful. Young couples were now eloping in hundreds, and stopped at his inn *en route* to Gretna Green with the monotonous regularity of a ticking clock.

But who was Benjamin Rudd to stand in the way of Cupid's arrow? He was there to earn a living and therefore eager to serve anyone who was willing to pay, and he who paid handsomest was served best. This, however, did not always chance to be in the couple's interest, for invariably the one to pay the highest price was whoever came chasing after, anxious to avert disaster and consequently prepared to reward the landlord well for any scrap of information he was able to divulge. It did occur to mine host that the couple above-stairs were a trifle old to be eloping, but consoled himself in the knowledge that the inevitable irate parent or brother would no doubt come galloping after them ere long, ready to ransom the lady's honour with the regular fee, plus the expense of repairs to his property should the customary duel ensue.

Meanwhile, upstairs in the private room much discussion and controversy was toward concerning the precise action which ought to be taken, but most important of all, who was to take it.

"There is only one solution to the problem, Nicholas," Diane was stating obdurately, seated at the rickety table upon which lay the requisitioned tray of food and drink—noticeably untouched—while the two discarded cloaks draped the bed. "You must return to Carnleigh Hall and escort Amelia hither whilst I await her."

" 'Pon rep, ma'am! I can't take m'self hence in this outlandish garb! Egad, I'd be the laughin' stock o' Carnleigh!" remonstrated Nicholas, pacing dementedly up and down the worn floor-boards, wringing his hands and chewing his bottom lip.

"No one will see you if you take the coach," she pointed out like a governess rebuking a small child, attired as she was in a simple gown of grey crape with white lawn trimmings, more suited to half-mourning and therefore conducive to her mood.

"But s'posin' y'r cousin an't willin'? S'posin' she refuses t' come?"

"Then you must do the obvious thing, Nicholas, and carry her off by force. You seem to have a genius for it."

"Ye gods! What about George? Damme, I'd ne'er escape alive!"

"You must make the effort, Nicholas," Diane insisted, losing patience. "After all, you are the one responsible for getting me into this deplorable mess, therefore, I do feel the onus lies with you to do the decent thing and try to get me out!"

"No! 'Pon oath, 'twasn't I! 'Twas all George's idea! Forced me! Threatened me! P-Please, Miss Winstone, at least c-come wi' me? I beg o' ye?" petitioned he in such wide-eyed frantic fear that Diane could almost have felt compassionate had not her own position been so critical. "George wouldn't dare t' run me through in y'r presence—"

"Oh no, Nicholas! Pray do not ask me," she faltered, averting her face to conceal her anguish. "Y-You really cannot expect m-me . . . to c-confront your elder brother again . . . i-it would be too m-much . . ."

Nicholas was suddenly overcome with excruciating shame and he ceased his pacing to hesitantly approach Diane, extending a nervous hand as if to touch her sympathetically, only to withdraw it again lest she misconstrue the gesture.

"Forgive me, Di—er—Miss Winstone. I'm exceedin' sorry. I hadn't realized the feelin'—hem—ran s' deep. O' course I'll—hum—go," he declared, bracing himself with shoulders squared like a soldier marching off to a battle from which he never expected to return. "Forsooth! 'Tis the very least I can do t' ease y'r burthen, ma'am."

Diane overturned a pathetic smile, extending her hand in gratitude.

"Thank you, Nicholas. I cannot tell you how relieved I should be if you would do as I ask." She made a brave attempt to rally herself. "Do not despair! There is every possibility that we have not yet been missed at Carnleigh Hall. Indeed, if you make haste you may arrive in time to save the day before the Earl even discovers we're gone."

Upon this score Nicholas cherished considerable doubt. Where vital matters were concerned, and other people's necks, George was not one to dally. And upon such an important issue as this he would have scarce allowed himself and Miss Winstone to reach the gates of the Lodge when he would have been blabbing everything into Quentin's attentive ear, and probably laying full blame upon his younger brother's plate. Paragon of self-control or not, Quentin would be furious—indeed, have every reason to be—but only until his adored Petronella saved the day by confessing the truth . . . that is, if George had yet seen fit to confide it to her.

"Well, Nicholas?" prompted Diane, trying to stem the urgency in her voice. "You appreciate that time is of the moment?"

Nicholas returned a piteous look. "A-A glass o' wine, p'raps? 'Odsbobs, ma'am, ye can't refuse a condemn'd man a glass o' wine?"

"As you wish," she sighed, filling a glass with the coarse red wine masquerading as a bottle of the inn's best burgundy. "But please, do make haste, Nicholas, or we shall never reach Thatcham this side of quarter-day."

Indeed, she had long harboured the belief that she and Amelia were not destined ever to reach Thatcham, and if they delayed much longer there would be little point in making the effort for Amelia's parents would be arriving home from Scotland.

As she served Nicholas with the wine she half suspected that it was requested merely as a means of delaying execution, and became convinced of this when his consumption of it turned out to take longer than she might have compassed the distance to Carnleigh on foot. It was as Nicholas finally drained the glass, unable to squeeze another droplet out of it, that the faint drum of hoof-beats was first to be heard through the open casement, to which neither paid any heed, for what was more commonplace than a mere horseman?

Meanwhile, Nicholas sought every subterfuge at his disposal to prolong his departure, and when he had redonned his cloak, tied the strings to his satisfaction with not one loop a fraction larger than the other, fidgeted with his hooped petticoat, and smoothed the wrinkles from his left stocking he eventually sidled towards the door, bowing his lachrymose adieux ere he finally slunk out of sight.

Diane hearkened to the sound of his footsteps slowly retreating down the creaking stair, not daring to credit that he had actually gone—whilst the hoof-beats grew louder, louder—drowning the hubbub in the yard below, until the horse came to an abrupt halt with a snort and a whinny, and an imperious voice called out:

"Ostler! My horse!"

With a long low rumble and a crash as the door burst wide Nicholas was back in the room, trembling from head to foot and his eyes starting from his head as if he had just collided head-long with the legendary Spectre of Carnleigh Wood.

"Q-Quen! It-It's Quen! Help, do something! S-Save me!" he gabbled wildly, scrambling under the table where he took refuge behind Diane's chair.

"D-Do calm-yourself, N-Nicholas," she endeavoured to compose him, though in need of a little composing herself. "There is n-nothing to f-fear. I-I shall not let any harm b-befall you."

Nicholas did not seem greatly reassured.

In the meantime, a vociferous exchange was in progress below—the authoritative voice of the Earl alternating with the sugary-obsequious tone of mine host, who was only too ready to indicate the room sheltering the truant pair in exchange for the five gleaming golden quineas his lordship flashed before his avaricious eyes. Soon, two pairs of feet were thudding up the stair, though it sounded like Cromwell's army, the eager stumping of mine burly host hastening as fast as his limbs would allow ahead of his illustrious patron whose lighter—though no less determined—tread could be heard echoing behind.

Diane could not find it in her heart to reproach Nicholas for feeling nervous. Indeed, although she had a deal less to fear than he she found herself struggling to suppress an overwhelming urge to scream as the steps thundered to a standstill immediately outside the door. Here, the landlord was curtly dismissed and was to be heard scurrying away back downstairs, followed by . . . silence!

She remained transfixed to her chair, scarcely daring to breathe, with nought to be heard but the sound of Nicky's babbled incantations as he tried to recall the catechism from his long-gone childhood. Even the friendly bustling out in the yard seemed to have suddenly ceased.

Sitting erect, Diane braced herself for the door to burst open and the Earl to rampage into the room brandishing his sword. But to her surprise the knob turned ever so slowly, and the door swung open quite soundlessly, so soundlessly in fact that Nicholas was as yet unaware that it had opened at all.

Lord Carnleigh's tall commanding figure stood framed in the doorway, his expression inscrutable as his cold grey eyes imbibed the pathetic little scene, one hand draped with lace resting ominously upon his sword.

Instinctively Diane rose to her feet and honoured him with a rather unsteady curtsy, for her legs trembled along with the rest of her, endeavouring to appear casual despite the agonising suspense which was draining her of strength, in the devout belief that a calm rational approach was her best weapon.

"Would you be pleased to enter, my lord?" she invited civilly, incurring a wail of alarm from Nicholas. "I can scarce own your arrival wholly unexpected," she appended, more for something to say as the deathly hush was unbearable.

In continued silence Lord Carnleigh entered the room, inclining his head in her direction which seemed to be all she could expect by way of greeting, closing the door behind him to stand, waiting, as if half prepared to hearken to their trumped-up excuses—though his hand still rested upon his sword.

"P-Perhaps you would care for some wine?" she suggested in an effort to humour him a trifle.

He acquiesced with a curt nod, and with trembling hands Diane managed to dribble some wine into the other glass which she then—as he evidently had no intention of venturing to the table—conveyed to him where he stood by the door. Granted, it was not a wine to command respect, neither did it receive it as the Earl consumed it in one draught then stood, alternately viewing the nervous pair through narrowed eyes, as if debating which to deal with first, and twirling the glass in his long tapering fingers.

"You probably come to seek some kind of explanation," she half-questioned, turning back to the table—

mindful the while to position herself protectively betwixt the Earl and his brother. "Would you believe it, my lord," she went on with a pitiful laugh, "but I actually mistook—"

"I would fain hear Nicholas first," he cut her dead.

"N-No, Quen! No! 'Twasn't I—'fore gad, I-I swear!" gasped Nicholas from his fortress. "G-George! 'Twas all George's idea! Told 'im ye wouldn't like it above half, but he wouldn't listen! B-Brooked no refusal, 'pon oath, Quen! F-Forced me t' dress m'self in Amelia's garb—"

"This would appear to be quite true, my lord," abetted Diane in earnest. "What motive could Nicholas possibly have for kidnapping me thus?"

The Earl's lips curled contemptuously as he placed the glass aside.

"You apparently do not yet know Nicholas as well as I, Miss Winstone," he observed, casting a significant glance towards the bed, registering some surprise to see the covers quite undisturbed.

Diane reddened profusely at the implication as Nicholas scrambled bravely out of his refuge—though on the farther side so that the table was conspicuously between his brother and himself.

" 'S death, Quen! What d'ye insinuate? Ye know deuced-well I've done wi' the petticoats! Told ye so a dozen times or more that I love only Petronella!"

"However, George thinks not," the Earl enlightened him, progressing gradually round the room in Nicky's direction—to Diane's disconcertment. "In fact, he swears just as devoutly that Miss Wilchards is nought but a coquette, a frivolous diversion from the true object of your desire . . ." His eyes revolved expressively in Diane's direction.

"I protest!" cried Nicholas. " 'Tis a monstrous lie!—er—y'r humble pardon, ma'am. No disparagement intended, by m' life—aye, m' very soul is devoted to Petronella, and if ye were t' bludgeon me t' the ends o' the earth I'd confess love for none other!"

This ardent declaration might have been enough to convince anyone less sceptical than the Earl of Carnleigh.

"Nonetheless," he returned with irony. "You must confess that Miss Winstone does not seem to be a damsel unduly distressed."

"And why should I be, my lord?" rejoined she resentfully. "I trust Nicholas whole-heartedly, as I should my own brother! And I realise that this entire episode is nothing but a boyish prank on George's part!"

The Earl reserved his judgement as he deposited himself upon a corner of the table where, to his companions' further alarm, he ominously drew his sword from its scabbard.

"Come here, Nicholas," he requested, quietly enough.

"I-I'm ex-exceedin' comf'table in m' p-present p-position, thank y-ye—"

"Nicholas?" persisted his brother in a harsher tone.

Diane swept across the room to intercept the two before blood could be shed.

"You shall not harm Nicholas, Lord Carnleigh!" she challenged him, her bosom heaving turbulently. "If you wish to kill him, you must first kill me!"

Virulence—or was it jealousy?—flashed momentarily in the Earl's grey eyes, and was gone.

"What kind of brother do you presume me to be, madam?" he rasped with scorn. "I have not the least

intention of harming him. There is nothing quite like a
brisk gallop for cooling a man's head!"

"Than would you be pleased to sheath your sword?"

"No, I would not be so pleased, Miss Winstone. In
fact, I'd be a deal better pleased if you would kindly
leave me to manage mine own affairs . . . Nicholas!"

Nicholas edged gingerly forward as if anticipating his
end despite his brother's assurance to the contrary.

"Y-Yes, Quen?"

"You were heard to threaten me earlier in the day,
so I am led to believe," his lordship informed him,
casting his expert eye along the weapon's deadly blade.
"Witnesses do amply testify that you actually threw out
a challenge—er—for philandering, is that the word?—
with Miss Winstone's affections."

Nicholas backed hastily. "I—I didn't mean it, Quen!
I *swear* I didn't mean it! 'Twas on the spur o' the moment! Ecod, s-spare me, I beg ye!"

Diane remained aside, her tension strung to breaking
point, her fingernails biting into the palms of her
hands, loth to interfere yet about to do so at any moment—when the Earl did something passing strange.

"Here, Nicholas, take my sword." He offered the
weapon hilt-first.

Nicholas swallowed hard shaking his fair head as he
backed even further away.

"Come, take it!" pressed his lordship, almost ge-
nially. "If I am the despicable scoundrel you think me,
then you may run me through here and now—"

"Gadzooks! N-Nay, Quentin!" he stammered in horror. "In truth, I ne'er meant . . . I ne'er termed ye
scoundrel. Never, damme!" He broke off, further
aghast to find that he had ripped a large hole in Amelia's gown. "I always deemed ye a gentleman o' the

highest d'gree, Quentin, a man o' honour. But t' give such an exhibit'n b' the fountain! Encouragin' a lady, just t' spurn her like a cast-off waistc't, gad! 'Tis nought short o' indecency . . . Er—me apologies, Miss Winstone, ma'am, but b' the faith, it must be said! And havin' said it, Quen, y're free t' strike me where ye will!"

"Pray, why should I have any desire to strike you, Nicholas, for merely speaking the truth?"

"Eh? Wh-What?"

"You are perfectly correct," approved the Earl, indolently toying with the weapon.

"I-I am?"

"Yes, I *was* philandering with Miss Winstone's affections—or so it would appear."

"Ye were?"

Nicholas flashed a bewildered glance at Diane to see how she was receiving this staggering confession.

"However, I must warn you," resumed my lord, the shrewd look intensifying in his eye. "If you uphold I shall die by the sword for such a wanton act, then 'tis reasonable to assume that Miss Winstone will meet similar fate, for she is guilty of the same crime."

"Zounds, Quentin! There ye go again, insultin' the lady!"

"I assure you, Nicholas that 'tis all perfectly true," affirmed the Earl with a cryptic smile. "As you do not choose to accept my word, then mayhap you will accept the word of Miss Winstone herself?"

"Is't true, ma'am?" probed Nicholas delicately, venturing two paces forward but keeping a weather eye on his brother. "Did ye philander with m' brother's affect'ns?"

Diane stiffened and turned away, wondering why

Lord Carnleigh had need of a sword when his tongue was almost as lethal.

"If he chooses to term it such, yes."

Nicholas returned his dumbfounded gaze to his brother.

"As I informed you in the library but a few hours since, Nicholas, the plan was agreed between us, to decieve George and yourself, just as George and you have sought to deccive Miss Winstone and myself. And in order to enact our roles—"

"Ye gods, ye don't still insist ye were acting'—b' the fountain?"

"Yes, Nicholas. Were we not, Miss Winstone?" he queried of her on a sardonic note.

It was all Diane could manage to nod her head, her back to the two.

"A-An' ye d-don't love . . . her?" faltered Nicholas dismally.

The Earl hesitated slightly. "Did I truly give that impression? Faith, I must be an even better dissembler than Miss Winstone."

Diane flinched as his arrow hit its mark, wondering why he was being so deliberately cruel. Surely he did not believe she had really intended to elope with Nicholas? That she actually loved him? For it almost seemed as if his cruelty were born of jealousy, an intense jealousy. Was it possible? Oh, how she longed, yearned, to believe it might be so.

"A-An' Miss Winstone?" pursued Nicholas in bitter disillusionment. "She doesn't love you, Quen?"

"No, Nicholas, though I can in no wise blame you for being deceived. 'S life, I was almost deceived myself. Indeed, a more convincing performance I have yet to witness."

Yes, Miss Winstone had certainly succeeded in deceiving himself and George, thought Nicholas, particularly upon the night of her arrival when she had declared herself to be their future sister-in-law. Or had she merely implied it, and they had leapt to the hasty conclusion?

"So everything has turned out advantageously," opined the Earl, finally sheathing his sword. "No one has been—er—inconvenienced . . . have they, Miss Winstone?"

"N-No, Lord Carnleigh," she replied, barely audibly.

"Er—unless Miss Winstone finds herself enamoured of you, Nicholas, which could prove somewhat awkward, especially when you claim so passionately to be already enamoured of another."

"Damme, Quentin! What d'ye inply b' that?"

The Earl regarded him curiously awhile, a look which irritated.

"I appreciate that George's word is not to be wholly relied upon, even so, he vowed most adamantly—er— on his very life and before heaven if I recall correctly, that you did carry Miss Winstone off by force, against her will and screaming for aid . . . though to be sure, I heard not a sound."

The Earl cast Diane a sidelong glance leaving her conscience to interpret this whichever way it felt inclined.

"Lies, damn 'im! All barefaced lies!" remonstrated Nicholas furiously, plummeting into brother Quentin's trap. "I swear with equal fervour, Quen, I ne'er touched her! Miss Winstone herself will tell ye!"

"Am I then to assume that the lady came willingly, Nicholas? Mayhap, even eagerly?" Lord Carnleigh parried calmly. "There is certainly no evidence to indicate otherwise. I vow when I entered just now the pair of you seemed far from hostile . . ."

Nicholas could have kicked himself for his stupidity and floundered nonplussed as Diane hastened to his rescue, and her own.

"I should never have agreed to such a thing, Lord Carnleigh!" she rounded on him, outraged. "I was under the impression that Nicholas was my cousin Amelia and that we were finally on our way to Thatcham—which I'd say looks perfectly obvious!"

"Aye, ye can't think I'd garb m'self thus for pleasure?" supported Nicholas, holding up his petticoats.

The Earl flung a disparaging glance all round. "You expect me to believe that you were actually deceived by this masquerade?" he questioned Diane, contemptuously. "A female gifted with your perception? Surely you know your own cousin sufficiently well to distinguish her from this merryandrew? Moreover, not a few moments since you did zealously volunteer your very life to protect him which, you must own, is scarce an act of indifference?"

"H-How dare ye, Quentin!" exploded Nicholas, storming up to his brother as if about to strike him but stopping short three feet away. " 'S death! I don't know what's got int' ye! The devil I don't! Ye seek t' read evil intent in the most innocent o' gestures, as if y'r deuced mind had warped round the edges!"

The Earl smiled, acknowledging this a compliment.

"I seek to protect Nicholas, Lord Carnleigh, because I feel in some way responsible for the dire predicament he is now in, and for no other reason!" Diane verbally attacked the Earl, her brown eyes, usually so mild and fawn-like, now flashing with flames in their depths.

"Had not I approached him upon that fateful night in the yard of The King Charles none of us would now be standing here!"

"How many times must I tell ye, Quentin, that my heart's sworn t' Petronella, an' that I'll love none other till the day I expire?" Nicholas furthered the avowal.

"Faith, Miss Wilchards at least appears to be convinced—your servant, mistress," drawled the Earl, bowing to the new arrival.

"Eh?" Nicholas spun round to see Petronella rushing towards him, arms outstretched, which was certainly not the way she had been schooled to enter a room occupied by gentlemen.

"Oh, Nicholas!" she cried, flinging herself into his bewidered arms. "I knew it was all a horrid trick, and that you truly still loved me!"

"Stap me, Petronella, it 'tisn't the second time ye've leapt out o' the very walls, m' love!" exclaimed Nicholas bemused with amazement, but no less overjoyed as he clasped her to his heart to reassure her of his love. "Zounds, how on earth—"

"My father forbad me to come," she panted breathlessly, trying to honour the Earl's bow with a curtsy despite Nicky's arms tightly round her waist. "My lord—Diane," she greeted them, then gushed on: "But I managed to outwit him upon pretext of adjourning to my room distraught with anxiety for your precious life—which I was of course, my darling Nicky! Quite, quite demented! Oh my dearest, are you hurt?" She flashed the Earl a look of venomous reproach. "Did your naughty wicked brother harm you?" she went on, searching Nicky's face for the least expression of discomfort, but the only discomfort Nicholas experienced

was the excruciating embarrassment of his female attire, and a degree of shock at mention of her father.

"Y-Y'r f-father? Gadswoons, h-he an't here?"

"Oh, Nicholas," she prattled gaily on. "Of all the
most wonderful things! He has given his word that we
may wed! Isn't that marvellous? He arrived a short
while ago and is this very moment at Carnleigh Hall
with—"

"Oh no he isn't ye minx!" came the blustering voice
of Sir Jason from the door, before he strode into the
room in no uncertain manner.

"F-Father!" gasped Petronella for the second time
that afternoon.

"We meet again, Wilchards," bowed the Earl, as Diane curtsied murmuring something incoherent and Sir
Jason kissed her proffered hand.

"Aha! Ye'll be Miss Winstone, I'm thinking—the
young lady who ran off wi' my future son-in-law, eh?"

Diane blushed painfully at the quip, but Sir Jason
had already turned away, demanding to meet the
young upstart who was the cause of all the upset.

"Well, minx! Sought to deceive me, eh? Thought
ye'd go gallopin' off to Scotland in place o' Miss Winstone here—Good gad! What's this?" he ejaculated
aghast upon espying Nicholas hovering behind his
daughter.

"Er—Nicholas, father," she ventured dutifully.

"Humph!" was all he could say, eyeing Nicholas dubiously up and down.

"Hem, the Hon-Honourable N-Nicholas—er—Ch-
Charles Durward—" stammered Nicholas like an idiot,
bowing in humble reverence.

"Ye can keep y'r string o' aristocratic names for the
vicar, m' boy," responded Sir Jason in gruff good-hu-

mour. "So this is the young rapscallion ye've set y'r heart on, is't?"

"Oh yes, father!" entreated Petronella ardently. "Please, you promised to give us your blessing."

"Hm-m, aye, well, p'raps we'd best go belowstairs and discuss this man to—hum—man," he suggested, obviously harbouring misgiving about Nicky's gender. .

Nicholas willingly seconded the proposal in order to escape from his brother's presence, despite the prospect of running the gauntlet of the local populace in the parlour and tap-room, garbed in his yellow muslin.

Loth to suffer the harrowing humiliation of being left alone in the Earl's company, Diane made to hasten after the three, alas, to find her path barred by my lord who, being nearer to the door, got there first, and closing it, stood with his tall arrogant back to it, confronting her—challenging her to effect an escape.

Seventeen

———◆—————

One glance up at the Earl's austere features and Diane turned away with a gasp of dismay, steeling herself against the raging tempest she sensed was to come though for precisely what, she was unable to determine. Personally, she considered she had come out of the whole wretched business worse than anyone, and had suffered quite enough for which she ought to be shown a modicum of sympathy, tolerance at the very least. Instead, he chose to be openly hostile—she knew not why and began to suspect he knew not either.

However, if Diane expected the Earl to act thus she erred somewhat in her judgement. On the contrary, his eyes dropped to some insignificant object upon the floor, he evidently finding it as difficult to meet her gaze as she was finding it to meet his.

"It is not my intention to detain you long," he ventured at last, labouring under strain and confusion, as if the experience were completely new to him. "There is something I would say yet know not . . . how to begin . . ."

Having said this he fell silent again, apparently wondering what he ought to say next and the precise words he ought to use, while Diane maintained the silence, her own embarrassment forgotten in favour of his, almost as confused as he, wondering if he were the same man, the same being who had so cruelly insulted her barely a moment ago. No longer did she see him as the impervious arrogant aristocrat, but as the true brother of George and Nicholas, a combination of them both—smouldering with aggression one moment as if he might throw caution to the winds and beat her senseless, and like a nervous ingenuous child the next, as if he were almost afraid of her.

"I have never before found myself in the unhappy position of having to apologise to anyone," he went on, his eyes roaming the ceiling with its knotted oak beams, the flaking walls, the bed, table, chairs, dresser, floor, up to the lattice, and back to the ceiling. "It is perhaps not surprising, therefore, that I find the relevant words eluding me . . . however, I can begin by apologising for the insults you have borne. I-I can think of no plausible reason why I should wish to offend you, or why you should see fit to pardon me. Nevertheless, I must crave your forgiveness . . . I have always prided myself upon my self-control . . ." He shrugged helplessly. "Why it should suddenly forsake me I am at a loss to understand." Again he broke off, now wandering up and down the sixteen foot room betwixt window and bed, leaving the door exposed for her to effect an escape, if she still so desired.

But Diane did not still so desire. Instead, she stood tensed, waiting for him to resume.

"You torment me as no other woman has ever done! I find to my abhorrence that I am no longer master of my thoughts and deeds, for I can think of nought else! Oft-times I know not what to do, for if I seek your company as my feeling dictate it plays the very devil with my self-discipline—yet, if I deny myself . . ."

She was now rooted to the floor whilst the Earl continued playing see-saw with her emotions, her face still averted but with eyes closed, biting her lip, her very heart, life, suspended from his words. Was this, at long last, the declaration of love she had desperately yearned for throughout the past agonising weeks? Was he in the process of unburdening his soul? Or was it all merely his over-elaborate way of apologising?

"Today, all was revealed to me concerning the night of your arrival, and the circumstances which prompted you to assume the role of my affianced," he stated with difficulty, as if the words were being torn from his body. "Obviously, I can now appreciate your reluctance to divulge the information to me, in order to protect my brothers. Though why you should wish to do so when they had used you so shamefully is beyond my comprehension. But fear not, ma'am, they will be made to atone for—"

"No! I implore you, Lord Carnleigh!" Diane besought him, her eyes consumed with anxiety. "Surely George and Nicholas have been punished enough? They were in desperate straits and were driven to desperate measures. I feel certain they would never have harmed my cousin and me. Even today, my lord, I am sure they both felt that they were acting in our best mutual interest in planning this elopement—being unable to accept the t-true . . . sit . . . uation."

Her eyes fell before his.

"I cannot conceive what they hoped to achieve by exposing you to such humiliation and condemnation on top of all else you have endured over the past months

. . . D-Diane," he breathed her name as he took her hands in his and raised them to his lips—her heart crying out: 'This is it! This is it! His confession of love!'—but alas, once again was Cupid's arrow off target. "I must beseech you to forgive us all—George, Nicky and myself—and to accept whatever I have to offer. Tell me, I pray you, in what manner I may atone for your suffering? You may have anything! You have been the instrument in attaining for me my dearest lifelong ambition, to see my brothers suitably married. Please, name your wish! You will not find me ungenerous, for my gratitude—"

"Gratitude!" she cried in anguish, snatching her hands out of his to flee to the window and gaze out with sightless eyes upon the distant horizon, her bosom heaving spasmodically with the turbulence within. No, not again! She could not withstand any more apologies nor gratitude! How could she tell him that *he* was her dearest wish? That his heart was the only thing which would cure her suffering?

Diane wrestled to suppress the tumult in her breast lest she ruin all by giving licence to it, for she stubbornly cherished the hope that a declaration of love would still be forthcoming from the Earl, if he could only be made to acknowledge the feeling. She remained frozen by the window, choking back the voice longing to make itself heard—shocked, appalled, to find that she was prepared to offer herself as his mistress if all else failed and this was the only alternative. How disgusted would be her strict punctilious relatives, Amelia's mamma and papa, and aghast at allowing their daughter to consort with one willing to so demean herself.

But her whole life was at stake, which weighed heavily against the conventional niceties. She needed him desperately. Wanted him more than anything in the world. And if this were the only relationship he would consent to, then yes, she would sacrifice her honour. That kiss! That fatal kiss which had awakened all manner of frightening passions within them both and opened their eyes to the realisation that their association would never be the same. It had utterly betrayed her, but it had utterly betrayed him too, proving that he was not as wholly indifferent to her as he professed to be.

If the Earl had caused Diane suffering hitherto, he was now inflicting upon her the most humiliating and painful task of all—that of plumbing the depths of his impenetrable heart and convincing him that the strange crucifying experience creating such chaos in his life was none other than that wonderful rare tender charism called love.

"May I ask why you came here, my lord?" she questioned suddenly, in a voice as distant as her gaze.

Curiosity flitted across my lord's handsome face. "Need you ask? Surely you are by now aware of Nicholas's reputation?"

"When you set out from your home, did you want to . . . h-harm him?"

A lengthy silence ensued ere he replied hoarsely: "May heaven forgive me—yes."

Diane inhaled deeply, striving to still her frantic heart.

"Did not you stop to ponder why your anger should be roused so bitterly against your brother? Why you should come galloping sword in hand prepared to do battle?"

"Obviously to protect your reputation and honour!"

"Which I do greatly appreciate, my lord," she acknowledged, turning to confront him. "But would you have reacted in similar manner had Nicholas eloped with Petronella? or anyone else? Would you have then felt so violently disposed towards him?"

She gripped the sill behind her, yearning for—yet equally dreading—his answer, whilst Lord Carnleigh weighed the question, viewing her strangely as he had done by the fountain.

"No," he responded at length, puzzled, as if this fact perturbed him. "I must admit, 'twould not have incensed me to any inordinate degree."

"Have you thought to ask yourself why?"

"Yes."

"And?"

My lord wandered round the table, toying with the items on the tray, trying to put aside his discomfort.

"If I might ask you a question, Miss Winstone," he parried her verbal thrust. "Why were you going to Thatcham—today?"

Diane gaped back at him, caught completely unawares, and a dull red suffused her cheeks.

"A-Amelia is now quite r-recovered . . . I-I saw no need to—to—delay our departure . . . any l-longer . . ." Her voice trembled away to an inarticulate squeak as he slowly advanced, his eyes holding hers in their unfathomable depths, until he was towering over her.

"Diane." He breathed her name as before but on a note of despair, his eyes deeply troubled. "Cannot your lively ingenuity concoct a more feasible excuse? Do you dislike my company so intensely that you must needs abandon my house like a thief in the night without a breath of farewell?"

"M-My Lord!" she choked on the outsized lump which had leapt to her throat. "I protest! That wasn't the reason at all!"

He was not convinced as he raised a hand to caress her cheek, decided against it, and forced a smile instead.

"Your wish, mistress," he chose to remind her, lightly. "You have not yet stated what boon you would crave in exchange for the excellent service you have rendered. Er—wealth, perhaps, that you might scorn the offer of every Jeremiah Figgis you chance to meet?"

"No! I can't endure any more!" she screamed finally losing her reason as the torrent of bitterness and heartache burst from her. "I don't want your apologies! I don't want your gratitude! And I certainly don't want your wealth!"

The Earl returned a bewildered stare, unable to comprehend this strange unpredictable creature before him, gazing up at his wild-eyed and distraught, obviously in need of something but not quite sure what.

"Faith, Diane," he murmured, hopelessly at a loss, "I have nought else to offer . . . except . . ."—he broke off, regarding her oddly askance, as if hardly daring to credit she might want that which he had in mind—". . . myself?"

Tears of joy and adoration glistened in her eyes as she held out her hands to him.

"Oh Quentin!" she sobbed with happiness. "How can a man as wonderful as you be so woefully blind?"

"I?—am your wish?" he queried stunned, unable to

grasp this wondrous miracle—until it suddenly struck him with all its force and he seized her into his arms on a tide of passion, straining her to him with a desperate yearning that nothing in the whole wide world—certainly no other female—could ever assuage, his lips craving hers with a desire almost frightening in its intensity, demanding everything she had to give and repaying her with something more vital to her existence—his love, his devotion, himself—whilst Diane returned his blazing ardour with an eagerness one might have thought born of much experience but for the fact that she had never kissed a man thus in her entire life. Clinging to him, frantic with yearning—afraid to let go lest he vanish before her eyes.

"Diane . . . Diane . . . how you have plagued my soul these weeks past," he breathed passionately, combing his long fingers through her hair to liberate it from its pins in all its cascading glory whilst his lips seared her neck. "There was I actually applauding myself upon my superb performance, wholly unaware that I had already quitted the stage and was no longer acting, which my accursed pride and self-discipline obstinately refused to acknowledge. I had no notion how much I loved you until today when I thought for one crucifying moment that you might love Nicky. And when I arrived to find you all but revelling in his company, not to mention leaping forth to sacrifice your very life for him, my darling, do you appreciate how close you came to being impaled by my sword to mine host's dilapidated floor-boards?"

Reverently he took her face between his hands to feast his eyes upon her beauty—enhanced a hundred-fold by that inner radiance generated by love which shone from her eyes as it had done upon that first occasion by the fountain.

"I've been a fool, Diane, a fool! I saw that same look in your eyes when I kissed you once before yet I was so overwhelmed by my own feelings that by the time I had recovered my senses it had vanished and all I could see was hatred, intense hatred, before you too vanished!"

"I-I thought you loved me in return, Quentin," she whispered deliriously. "So much was revealed in that k-kiss . . . then I realised you were only acting—"

"No, beloved one! It was at that precise moment I realised I wasn't! I was bewildered, lost; you left me floundering in a sea of confused emotions—which was what I deserved for being so blind, so brack-brained! George recognised it, Nicky too! Yet I, so quick to criticise others," he murmured against her lips, "remained senseless, impervious to the most precious gift a man can merit." And again he gave evidence of his overwhelming love.

Thus it endured, until Diane's head fell onto my lord's shoulder in blissful contentment whilst the world, including The Jingling Jester and its patrons, passed them by.

"You force a hard bargain, my love," sighed my lord anon. "You would have me as well as my apologies, gratitude and wealth."

"No, Quentin . . . only yourself," she smiled up at him coquettishly, playing havoc with his equilibrium.

"Er—which reminds me of something else I have to offer," he ventured hesitantly.

"Not your horse?" she parried sober-faced.

"No, my dear girl, that you shall *never* have! However, you may have my name, as you so wish."

Diane twisted in his arms to regard him in wide-eyed innocence.

"Are you proposing, my lord?" she queried with a disconcerting directness.

"I am, Miss Winstone," he replied in like manner. "Faith, 'twould be an excellent theme for Sunday sermon, would it not? Snare not thine brothers in wedlock lest thee thyself be snared."

His future Countess lapsed into uncontrollable mirth.

"Oh, Quentin," gasped she at length, "it really ought to teach you a lesson!"

"Nonetheless, a lesson I trust I shall enjoy . . ." he responded, a wicked twinkle in his eye which evoked a girlish blush to his betrothed's cheeks as he guided her over to the window to look down into the inn-yard to see it strangely full of activity once again.

Yes, there were Sir Jason, Petronella and Nicholas standing by the coach, apparently with everything conveniently settled if the beaming smiles and hearty laughter were aught to go by and the paternal hand Sir Jason was clapping upon Nicky's shoulder.

"Hm, it appears to augur well for Nicky and his chambermaid, dear one."

"Indeed so, Quentin," Diane readily agreed—to heave a plaintive sigh. "I wish I might think it augured as well for George. He has yet to face Amelia's parents—"

"And he has yet to face me!" cut in the Earl with emphasis.

"Please don't be too severe with him, Quentin? After

all, his plan has proved a resounding success, has it not?"

"That I grant. But he has yet to answer for the first occasion!"

Here, the unmistakable feet of Nicholas were heard rumbling and stumbling up the stairs before he burst into the room.

" 'Swoons, Quentin! Are ye plannin' t' stay the night? Damme, Miss Winstone will ne'er get to—eh? Oh!—ahcm . . ." he tailed off upon spying his brother by the window with the lady in his arms.

"Weren't you ever taught to knock before bursting into a room unannounced, Nicholas?" enquired the Earl languidly.

"Thunder an' turf, don't tell me!" he grinned all over his face. "Miss Winstone won't be goin' t' Thatcham."

"No, Nicholas, not today," concurred the Earl, affably. "Miss Winstone has done me the unprecedented honour of consenting to be my wife—"

"Ecod! Not again!" came the deflating response. "Curse it, Quen! Ye an't still play-actin'?"

"No, Nicky," replied his lordship, raising his future bride's hand and planting a gentle kiss in its palm, his eyes never deviating from hers. "This time, we are pledged in all truth."

Nicky's face sparkled with joy as he dashed away downstairs to spread the news—without even pausing to offer his second round of felicitations.

Meanwhile, Diane turned to her noble lord. "If I am not yet travelling to Thatcham, Quentin, I really ought to inform Amelia's aunt of our whereabouts. Goodness knows what she'll be thinking."

"I doubt if that will be necessary, my love," returned

the Earl blandly. "I took it upon myself to allay the dowager lady's fears on that score some time agone."

"Y-You did?"

"I deemed it politic in order to avoid a public outcry and full investigation, with the tipstaff and his band of constables skulking behind every bush. You must confess, my own, that we shall have sufficient to endure when news of our forthcoming nuptials spreads abroad," my lord enlightened her, taking her arm to guide her to the door. " 'S life, I am loth to think what my good friends Digsey and Weldon will have to say when they discover I am about to wed one of my own kitchenwenches."

Diane giggled irrepressibly. "It will certainly require some explaining. Not to mention the outbreak of small-pox and, of course, the horse!"

The two paused by the door to take a final affectionate glance round the humble little room where so much had happened to transform their lives.

"Aye," opined the Earl, turning to descend the stairs with his newly affianced on his arm. "However, it has adamantly decided me about one thing!"

"The horse, my lord?"

"Indeed, my love," he returned without the vestige of a smile. "I am resolved henceforth, never as long as I live, shall I consume another Michaelmas pie."

* * *

It is perhaps not surprising that the journey back to Carnleigh was an exceedingly jovial affair, so much so, that before the coach had travelled many miles my Lord Carnleigh was quite willing to forgive George his misdemeanours—as all had turned out so prodigiously well for everyone concerned—whilst Nicholas could scarcely contain his feverish excitement to break the astounding news of the double wedding to come about in the Shadwick household.

However, it was to be remembered that a very dubious George had been left behind at the house. After all, how could he be absolutely certain that his scheme would work out as planned? Furthermore, he did not like at all the mood in which brother Quentin had ridden off to rescue his damsel—nor the way he had threatened him with blood and brimstone upon his return if he found him out in as much as the breath of a lie! On the contrary, now that George had ample time to ponder the situation he could not truthfully envisage Quentin's rage allowing him to pay heed to his heart and clasp Miss Winstone in his arms, breathing amorous proposals of marriage in her ear, as he (George) intended he should.

And what of Nicky's fate? This, also, was George extremely loth to reflect upon for the more he did so the blacker it appeared.

Far be it from anyone's deliberate intention to pronounce the Honourable George Shadwick, craven, as Petronella had done, but there suddenly occurred to him the most ingenious plan he had ever conceived, whereby he could evade the wrath of my lord, Amelia's parents, and do himself a service into the bargain. Indeed, it was such an obvious solution that he marvelled how he had not thought of it earlier!

Consequently, upon his return to his country seat, the Earl of Carnleigh found George nowhere to be seen, little realising until some time later that his conniving brother was well on his way to making a triple-alliance in the Shadwick family, for he and his doting Amelia had seized their chance during everyone's absence—and eloped.

It would be doubtful if the precise moment was ever established when George eventually discovered that his wife was, after all, an extremely wealthy heiress . . .

Romantic Fiction

If you like novels of passion and daring adventure that take you to the very heart of human drama, these are the books for you.

☐ AFTER—Anderson	Q2279	1.50
☐ THE DANCE OF LOVE—Dodson	23110-0	1.75
☐ A GIFT OF ONYX—Kettle	23206-9	1.50
☐ TARA'S HEALING—Giles	23012-0	1.50
☐ THE DEFIANT DESIRE—Klem	13741-4	1.75
☐ LOVE'S TRIUMPHANT HEART—Ashton	13771-6	1.75
☐ MAJORCA—Dodson	13740-6	1.75

A-20

Jean Plaidy

"Miss Plaidy is also, of course, Victoria Holt." —PUBLISHERS WEEKLY

☐ BEYOND THE BLUE MOUNTAINS	22773-1	1.95
☐ CAPTIVE QUEEN OF SCOTS	.23287-5	1.75
☐ THE CAPTIVE OF KENSINGTON PALACE	23413-4	1.75
☐ THE GOLDSMITH'S WIFE	22891-6	1.75
☐ HERE LIES OUR SOVEREIGN LORD	23256-5	1.75
☐ LIGHT ON LUCREZIA	23108-9	1.75
☐ MADONNA OF THE SEVEN HILLS	23026-0	1.75

Buy them at your local bookstores or use this handy coupon for ordering:

A-33